"You're wa... someone,...

Lachlan's que... ...e silence between them.

"It's sure as dammit not *you*," she breathed.

"Isn't it?" Lachlan said softly. "It would have been—years ago."

"No!" She couldn't bear that. That was unforgivable. He had said what should never have been said. "No!" She shook her head to make the words go away and her hair tumbled around her face. She put her hands up to shut out the sight of him, but he pulled them away.

He said harshly, "Oh, yes, Catriona. Don't you know why I left Crannich? It was because of *you*...."

She was trembling, helpless and vulnerable. She felt as if she couldn't breathe—she wanted to run away. Dear God...he, too, remembered. She had been wrong about that.

"You've never forgotten, have you, Catriona?"

MARY WIBBERLEY
is also the author of these

ℋarlequin Presents

and these

Harlequin Romances

Many of these titles are available at your local bookseller.

For a free catalogue listing all available Harlequin Romances
and Harlequin Presents, send your name and address to:

HARLEQUIN READER SERVICE,
M.P.O. Box 707, Niagara Falls, NY 14302
Canadian address: Stratford, Ontario N5A 6W2

MARY WIBBERLEY

a dream of thee

Harlequin Books

TORONTO • LONDON • LOS ANGELES • AMSTERDAM
SYDNEY • HAMBURG • PARIS • STOCKHOLM • ATHENS • TOKYO

Harlequin Presents edition published March 1981
ISBN 0-373-10419-7

Original hardcover edition published in 1980
by Mills & Boon Limited

CHAPTER ONE

CATRIONA was walking in the woods with Simon. It was one of those beautiful autumn days when it was actually not raining, and Simon said, in his usual authoritative way: 'You know, Kate, I can see it all now, those dreary cottages spruced up, that ghastly jetty replaced with a new one, a craft shop where that tatty old mill is now——'

Catriona was only half listening. Simon's enthusiasms were legendary, his money guaranteed success in anything he chose to do, and he'd only been here half a day and was already replanning the island. She let him ramble on, nodding, adding a comment in all the right places, but, remembering Crannich as it had been so many years ago.

She had left there at eighteen and gone to live in London, and life had changed dramatically, practically overnight. This had once been her home and she had loved it, but she was as much a stranger here now as Simon. She didn't belong here any more. Perhaps she never had. But she had been unable to ignore the plea of her elderly grandparents, her only relatives, and she had returned to stay after seven years——

'Kate! You're not listening,' he said accusingly.

'Sorry.' She gave him a cool little smile. 'I was thinking.'

'Hmm. I know you were born here, my love, but really, you don't intend to *stay*, do you?'

'For a week or two, that's all, I promise. My grandparents have never asked me to come home before quite so strongly——'

'Home?' His expression barely hid his contempt. 'My love, you no more belong here than I do!'

'But you're planning to buy those cottages, the old mill——'

'Not to stay here myself, for God's sake.' He laughed. 'Heaven forbid! I'll come up in the beginning, just to start it off, of course, but I'll get Ned on it then. I'll make a packet. All the trendy Hampstead types who can't wait to get away and try the simple life for a week or two—especially if I advertise it right, imply it's the "in" thing—you wait!'

'You're a cynical swine,' she commented. God, she was tired. If their letter hadn't come, she would have had to get away somewhere, anywhere, for a week——

'Aren't I just? And you wouldn't have it any other way, would you, my precious?' He gave her a smile that barely escaped a leer. 'You're my kind of person, Kate—let's face it. And you no more care about this stagnant backwater than I do. It'll wake the people of this little island up all right. Give 'em something to do, instead of just idling their time away fishing.'

'My grandparents live here, remember?' she said tartly.

'Sure they do. And they're dear people. But they're old. They're quite happy in that big house —it's well away from the village. It won't bother them. You know, I might even open up some kind of health farm here——'

'Over my dead body,' said a voice, and a man stepped out of the trees to the side of them. Simon stared hard, as if trying to locate the source of an unpleasant smell, and Catriona stared too—and felt her heart pound erratically, and the blood rush to her face. If Simon had not had hold of her arm, she might have fallen. The man, quite unmistakably, all six foot three of him, was Lachlan Erskine. A man she had thought, and hoped, she would not see again.

'And who the devil are you?' demanded Simon.

Lachlan walked forward. His black hair was as shaggy as ever, he wore faded jeans and a fisherman's jersey that needed one elbow darning, and he looked like a disreputable layabout—except for his face. The thick black eyebrows, the deep-set eyes, straight broad nose, wide mouth and square chin were anything but disreputable. He looked extremely hard, tough—and aggressive. 'I'm Lachlan Erskine,' he answered. 'You're Simon Meredith—and she's Catriona Forbes, late of this island, now of London, well-known actress, darling of the TV screens, chat shows, and jet-setting trendies. Is that where you're from?'

'That's none of your damned business.' Simon turned to Catriona. 'Do you *know* this man?' He asked it in tones which implied that she might have warned him if so.

Catriona looked coldly at Lachlan. 'He used to live here, years ago. The same as I did,' she answered. Her green eyes clashed with his hard grey ones, and Simon might not have been there. The memories were strong. She hated him ...

'It's no surprise you're with him,' Lachlan said to her. 'I should have known you'd bring trouble when you returned.'

She felt her temper rising, but quelled it. That was what he wanted, to see her make a fool of herself—of course! Just like last time. She was older now, and wiser, no longer the naïve girl from the island. She smiled instead.

'And what are you doing?' she asked calmly. 'Slumming?'

'No, living here.' His tone was deadly, his voice quiet.

Simon, puzzled, angry, looked from one to the other. He was usually in charge of every situation, but this was beyond him. 'Would you mind telling me,' he said, in tones as deadly as Lachlan's, 'what this is all about?'

'I'll tell you on the way home,' she answered.

'Never mind that, I'm not going anywhere until you explain what you meant by "over my dead body",' said Simon, glaring at Lachlan in a way that guaranteed wilting in practically everyone he had opposition from.

Lachlan merely laughed. He wasn't supposed to have done that. He was supposed to look embarrassed, or glance away. Instead he came nearer.

'I'll explain all right,' he said, and looked Simon slowly up and down. 'It means that I don't like your fancy ideas for craft shops and health farms and crowds of people rushing about bleating how marvellous it is to be staying on this quaint little island——' he stopped, turned to Catriona and smiled. 'And you'd better tell him that I always get my own way.'

She caught her breath, shaken, and moved fractionally away. 'Leave it, Simon,' she said. 'You won't get anywhere with *him*.' She injected as much scorn as she could manage into the last word.

Simon was not to be humoured. He shook her arm free. 'Won't I?' She saw the danger signs in his face, the tightening of the skin round his mouth, the way his eyes narrowed, and she wanted to warn him. He wasn't in London now, and he wasn't dealing with the usual kind of people he dealt with, and while he too was tough and strong, he hadn't encountered a man like Lachlan before, because if he had, he wouldn't have forgotten it. Catriona hadn't forgotten him, and it had been some years since she had last encountered him ...

'Listen here, Erskine, I don't take kindly to people eavesdropping on my private conversations for a start. So why don't you push off and go back to your fishing, or whatever it is you do, there's a good fellow, because there's nothing *you* can do to stop *me* doing precisely what I want, and if I wasn't serious before I would be now, because those cottages, and that mill, are for sale, and because no one, but no one, tells me what to do or what not to do. Savvy?'

'You pompous idiot,' grinned Lachlan, amused.

Too late, Catriona saw Simon's hand going up. She tried to stop him, but was pushed aside as Simon launched himself forward, face blazing red. Nobody had ever dared to call him pompous—not to his face anyway—and no one in their right mind would ever had said he was an idiot. Lachlan had just done two unforgivable things.

Thud! Simon's fist connected, not with Lachlan's jaw but with his upraised forearm, his left forearm. His right came out with the speed of light, and Simon seemed to leap backward, arms flailing, before crashing into the undergrowth, where he lay sprawling.

'Oh dear,' said Lachlan mildly and with apparent satisfaction. 'Did he fall over?'

'You beast!' Furious, unheeding, Catriona launched herself on the man who was just about to suck his knuckles, and swung her bag at his face. He caught it, wrenched it from her, and took hold of both her hands. His eyes gleamed darkly as he looked down at her.

'Careful,' he warned. 'You don't want to hurt yourself, do you?'

'Let me *go!*' She tried to pull away, but he

pulled her towards him and held her helpless
against his chest.

'Fiery as I remember,' he said softly. 'Fiery
Catriona of the red hair and green eyes——'

'You—you——!' She glared at him, eyes blazing
fury, and kicked his leg, and heard, from somewhere in the background, a muffled groan as
Simon came round. But it didn't seem to matter.
There might have been only two of them in that
dark, overgrown place. Only the two of them, as it
had been once, long, long ago ...

She remembered, and shivered inwardly, and
Lachlan released her, as if he too remembered.
'Take him back,' he said abruptly. 'Because I don't
want to see him again. Just tell him it doesn't pay
anyone to tangle with me.'

He turned away and vanished into the trees as
Simon staggered to his feet. 'I'll kill the b——' he
began.

Catriona held him. 'Ssh!' she said. 'He's gone.
Let's go back.'

'The coward!' He stroked his jaw carefully,
wincing. 'That was a lucky blow he landed—which
way did he go? I'm going to give him the thrash-
ing——'

'You'll not find him,' she said. 'He's used to these
woods. Don't you see? He must have followed us—
and we didn't even know.'

'He's mad! The man's a lunatic. My God!—
You *knew* him—and you didn't warn me?'

'*I* didn't know,' she said, stung by his tone. 'How

could I? I've not seen him for——' she hesitated—
'years. I didn't know *he* was staying here.' Or I
wouldn't have come back myself, she added silently.
But she couldn't tell Simon that, or he would want
to know why. 'We'd better go home and I'll put
something on your chin. Look—er——' She hesitated. How to tell Simon not to try anything physical with a man like Lachlan, without making him
more determined to sort him out? Simon was extremely proud of his fighting prowess, a good
amateur boxer, rugby player and keep-fit en-
thusiast. 'Er—if I were you, I'd keep out of Lachlan's way. He was well known for being—er—a bit
rough in the old days.'

'Are you trying to tell me he's stronger than
me?' Simon demanded, furious, eyes on her, contempt filled.

I'm damned sure he is, unfortunately, she
thought. 'No, not that—but you fight fair, and I'll
bet he wouldn't,' she answered. The lie seemed to
appease him, for the moment anyway. He grunted
something, she went to pick up her bag, found that
the strap had snapped, and they set off back to her
grandparents' home.

That was only the first shock. The second and
greater one came later that day. They had not
mentioned the encounter with Lachlan to Catriona's grandparents, and it was only when they
were sitting round the dinner table that night that
her grandfather said:

'How long will you manage to stay with us, Catriona?' He smiled gently at her across the table. A tall man, slightly stooped now, well into his seventies, with a shock of white hair and weather-beaten complexion, he looked a figure of health, as did her grandmother, who was busily employed in helping herself to green beans, and who paused spoon in mid-air, as if waiting for Catriona's reply.

She smiled at them. Simon's dignity had been restored, his ruffled feathers smoothed down, and the atmosphere was calm again. Catriona loved them. She regretted her long absence—now that she was here. She had thought of them often in London in the midst of her busy life, and had telephoned them every week and come up occasionally, but their importance had faded in the light of new excitement, new friends, constant adulation . . .

'I'll try and stay for a week or so,' she answered. 'Simon has to go back on Monday, of course, but I'm between jobs at the moment, and I badly needed a break. It's so peaceful here.' But I couldn't stand it for more than a week, she thought. I don't belong here any more.

'That's nice, dear,' her grandmother said. 'Simon, some beans for you?'

'Please, Mrs Forbes.' Simon took the dish from her. He could be very charming when he chose, and he was choosing to be so now. Catriona knew why. He intended finding out all he could about the cottages, and the mill. 'Thank you. This is a wonderful house, full of character. Catriona described it to me, of course, but I must say the reality exceeds my expectations.'

'Ah,' said Mr Forbes. 'But it's getting too much for us now, I'm afraid. Much too big.' He looked at his wife who looked back at him and, it seemed to Catriona, gave a slight, warning shake of her head.

'Well, never mind,' she said briskly. 'I'm sure Simon and Catriona don't want to hear about our problems. Potatoes, Simon?'

'Please. Delicious food. You grow all your own vegetables, don't you?'

'We do,' Mr Forbes beamed. Gardening was his hobby. Simon couldn't have done better if he'd been primed by Catriona. She could relax, and let the conversation ebb and flow round her. She wondered where Lachlan was living. In his old house? She would avoid it, and him, scrupulously, while she was there. She needed a rest anyway. There was plenty of space on the island to take gentle strolls without having to encounter him.

'Sorry?' She realised that her grandmother was speaking to her.

'I said old Mrs Grant died last month. Her house is up for sale.'

'Oh, I'm sorry about that. She was about ninety, wasn't she?'

'Ninety-five. She'd had a good life, mind, active to the end.'

'Did you say her house was up for sale?' asked Simon, injecting a respectful, sorry-about-Mrs

Grant note to his voice, but clearly determined to get the conversation round to where he wanted. 'Would that be one of the cottages that's for sale down by the shore?'

'Why, no, they've been for sale for a while. There's no sign put up yet in hers. It's alone, past those six. So many people move away, you see.' Mrs Forbes clicked her teeth. 'Aye, it's a shame right enough, but that's progress for you. There's no money here, you see, any more. Since the old woollen mill closed there's no work either.'

'And that's for sale as well?'

'Aye, it is.' Mr Forbes gave him a shrewd look. 'You'd not be interested, would you now?'

Simon laughed, a modest, unassuming laugh. He did that well, Catriona thought. 'Heavens, it'd be more money than I can afford, I dare say.' You liar, she thought.

'Och, I don't know,' Mr Forbes said thoughtfully. 'We've a brochure on it somewhere that says the price—it's not much they're asking—there's no demand, you see.'

'I'd appreciate a look later.' Simon gave him a winning, boyish smile.

'Aye, well, remind me to look it out, Mary.'

'I will, dear,' his wife replied. 'Tell me, Simon, what would you want with an old mill?'

'Well, it could be opened as a craft shop,' he answered.

'That it could. But who would you sell to? We get very few tourists here.'

'Well, I'll be perfectly frank with you, Mrs Forbes. I was mentioning to Catriona today that it seemed a shame to see so many houses empty, and I've a lot of friends in London who would love to get away for odd weekends, somewhere quiet like this—away from the hustle and bustle you know.'

'Ah, you'd buy the houses too, and rent them out, you mean?' Ian Forbes asked, as if interested.

'Something like that. It's only an *idea*, of course —at the moment.'

'It would bring life back to the community,' said her grandfather slowly, 'but would it work out?'

'I'd go into all that. I'd have to see round there first, and get an idea what state they were in.'

'I don't like it,' Mary Forbes said firmly. 'No disrespect to you, Simon, but we like our island as it is.' She looked at him. 'You see, you're a stranger here. You don't know our ways.'

'No, but I'd like to,' he answered. 'It's so peaceful—so beautiful,' He gave her a smile calculated to melt a heart of stone. 'Could you not share that beauty with others?'

'Now, Mary, you mustn't be hard on him. What will he think of us, eh?' said Mr Forbes, and she turned her gaze on him. White-haired, rosy-cheeked, she looked gentle and soft, and Catriona suppressed laughter. She was a match for anyone if she chose to be—probably even Lachlan. Which was a strange thought for Catriona to have, especially in the light of her grandmother's next words.

'Lachlan wouldn't like it either,' she said, unaware that it was like waving a red flag in front of an enraged bull to mention that name in front of Simon, whose hand went up instinctively to his jaw.

'Lachlan?' he said softly. 'Would he be the man we met today, Catriona?' Soft and dangerous, his voice, and he looked at her.

'Yes,' she answered.

'Oh, you've met him?' Mary Forbes' blue eyes were on Simon, shining with innocence.

'Yes, we met him,' he said. He put down his knife and fork. 'He—met us in the woods and told us—we were talking, and he must have overheard —that he didn't like the idea. But I fail to see what business it is of his, quite frankly.'

Ian Forbes cleared his throat. 'Aye, well, he has the keys for the properties, you see.'

Catriona froze. He had what?

'Is he the seller?' Simon's face was a picture.

'I believe he's acting for an agent who's dealing with the houses. So you'd have to see him first.'

'Does he live here?' Simon asked.

Again the look passing between the old couple, and again it was Mrs Forbes who answered. 'He's come back to live for a while,' she said gently. 'He grew up here.'

'Doesn't he work?' Catriona couldn't speak. She was leaving it all to Simon. But she wanted to know as well as he.

'Oh yes,' Mrs Forbes smiled. 'Oh yes, indeed.'

'What at? Surely there's nothing much to be

earned fishing.'

'Oh, he's not a fisherman!' She laughed merrily. 'Though I dare say he dresses like one.' It was almost as if Simon was having to fight for every scrap of information, a fact of which he seemed only too well aware. Catriona gave him credit for that. He had a quick temper, but was controlling it superbly well. It was also, she thought a moment later, as if her grandmother was enjoying the situation. Considering that their letter to her had been a desperate plea for her to go and see them because their health was failing, it was also a surprise. She had never seen them looking more robust. She watched, and listened to what had assumed the proportions of a battle of wits between the two, the elderly woman and the young hard-headed, wealthy businessman. The grandmother's face was a picture of innocent amusement.

'What is he, then, Mrs Forbes?' Simon asked gently. He might well go outside afterwards and let out a roar of frustration, but here and now, all was placid on the surface.

'Why, I believe he writes plays, doesn't he, Ian?' She beamed at her husband, missing Simon's barely concealed snort of disbelief.

'Plays? A playwright?' Simon echoed. 'How interesting! For amateur groups, you mean?' He hid the sneer well. Catriona could see it, but then she knew him better than they did.

'Oh no, dear. At least he might do that as well, I dare say. But he's been working in London for a long while,' Catriona felt as if she would faint. London. *He* had been in London—dear Lord, Lachlan Erskine, in *London*!

'I go to a lot of plays, in my job,' Simon told her. He was enjoying this now. His confidence had been fully restored. He was shortly going to do a demolition job on Lachlan Erskine, and he was looking forward to it. 'But I've never heard the name Lachlan—what's his other name? Erskine—before.'

'Well now, you wouldn't have. He doesn't write under his own name, does he, Ian dear? What *was* the name he told us?'

Both of them, Simon and Catriona, waited to hear the answer. But for different reasons.

Mr Forbes snorted with laughter. 'You've forgotten, Mary? Shame on you! And it the name of one of Scotland's most famous men in history.' He looked at them. 'His pen name, as I believe you call it, is Robert Bruce.'

Stunned, silenced, Catriona and Simon looked at him. Shock waves hit her with the force of a physical blow. Robert Bruce—one of the most successful playwrights of the past decade, with three plays running to packed houses in London's theatreland, was none other than the man she loathed, Lachlan Erskine.

CHAPTER TWO

Simon, white-faced, paced up and down the neat rows of growing vegetables. 'I don't believe it,' he muttered. He glared at Catriona as if she were to blame. 'And you mean to tell me you didn't know?'

'How could I?' she retorted angrily. 'How the hell would *I* know?'

'You're a bloody actress,' he answered.

'So? I'm on television. He doesn't write for TV. I've never met him at any parties. Don't you think I'd have remembered if I had?' The shock had been as great—if not greater—for her.

'He's lying. He's spun them a yarn—that—that *thug* we met today couldn't write a play to save his life. Where does he live?' Simon looked round as if a house might appear.

'What do you mean? You're going to *see* him?' she gasped.

'Yes, I damned well am. I have to, about the cottages as well, don't I?'

'Do you think he'll give *you* the keys to view?'

'He can't refuse. Not if he's acting as agent—— Agent, hah! Oh, sure, all famous playwrights go round touting for estate agents in their spare time. *Where's his house?*' he finished fiercely.

'Don't try and boss me, Simon,' she warned. 'I'm

not one of your women, remember?'

He softened fractionally. 'Sorry. But people like him get me so mad.'

'So I can see. And if you march in like that you'll get a dusty reception.'

'All right, I'll calm down. I've seen the vegetables now, let's go for that walk we're supposed to be going on. I can't see a damned thing anyway, it's getting too dark. Just lead me to his house. I'll be civilized.'

'You say that now——' she began.

'I will be. I'm going to expose him for the fraud he is.'

'What if he really *is* Robert Bruce?'

His lip curled. 'Come off it! Robert Bruce is probably whooping it up at some Chelsea party right now. Your Lachlan Erskine might have met him—but I'll bet a fiver that's the nearest he's ever got to a writer.'

'All right. It's this way.' Catriona turned and led him away from the big old house. The light shone out from the living room, where her grandparents were watching television. It was the set she had bought for them three years ago, when she had been in her first play on TV. Reception wasn't easy, but they had an extra booster on the roof aerial, and watched happily every evening. Down the overgrown driveway and out to the narrow track from the village, and Catriona led him away from there, then they began to climb slightly, following the curve of the coastline up a stony track that petered out, and there in front of them, perched on the sloping cliff top, was a large two-storey cottage. A light shone at a window and smoke curled up from the chimney.

It was at that moment that Catriona realised she didn't want to go any further. She stopped, and Simon turned impatiently. 'Come on,' he said. 'Why have you stopped? Scared?'

'No, let's leave it. I'll find out all about those cottages for you, and the mill.'

He turned, slowly, looked at her, his face a pale blur in the strong moonlight. 'You probably will,' he said. 'But that's not why you want to back out, is it?' He laughed. 'I think you don't want to see lover boy's face when he knows I'm on to him.'

She felt herself flush. 'Don't call him lover boy,' she said icily. 'I can't stand the man—I just don't want to be part of your little scheme to humiliate him.'

'He tried to humiliate me today,' he said softly, dangerously. 'And why can't you stand him? You never did tell me that.' He stood there waiting for an answer, but he wasn't going to get it. There were some things too deep and too personal ever to tell anyone. Catriona shook her head.

'No particular reason,' she said lightly. 'A slight —family feud when I was younger. Nothing that would interest you.'

'That's odd. Why is he so pally with your grandparents, then?'

'Good heavens, it was years ago. Besides, they're

not the kind to bother, they're too old.' He
grunted, bored with the subject, wanting only to
get on to the house.

'I'm going on my own if you're not coming, it's
up to you,' he said. And he meant it. Catriona hesitated, then decided. She didn't want them to fight,
and anything was possible with Simon—and Lachlan, whose temper had been hair-trigger fast, years
ago. They wouldn't fight if she were there.

'I'll come,' she said. 'But please——'

Simon turned away and walked on. Catriona,
after a moment, followed him. She was spoilt,
because everyone spoiled her. Even Simon, who
loved her as much as he was capable of loving
anyone, and in London she only had to crook her
finger for people to come running—but here, now,
today, he had changed. He wasn't going to obey any
whims of hers. Not now, at this moment.

She stumbled up the rough ground behind him,
and he was already knocking on the door when she
caught up. There was a brief silence following the
thunderous clap of the knocker, and the door was
opened, and Lachlan stood there, clad the same as
he had been that morning, the light flooding out
from behind him.

'Come in,' he said. 'I was expecting you,' and he
stood aside.

The door opened directly into a large living
room, with two doors leading off. A fire blazed up
the chimney, and the furniture was old and shabby,
but comfortable-looking. A television stood in one

corner and several books lay on the settee. The floor had on it a threadbare carpet, an indeterminate shade of brown, faded and worn. Lachlan picked up the books and put them on the table, which still bore evidence of a meal, a plate, a salt pot, knife and fork, tea mug.

'Sit down,' he said. He looked at them both, and Catriona met his eyes coolly. The angry man of the morning was gone and he looked calm, almost amused.

'I won't sit, thank you,' said Simon. His voice was the one he used when dealing with difficult clients in his advertising agency. Smooth, bland, giving not an inch. 'We won't be here long. I've just come to ask you if you'll let me have the keys to view the cottages.'

Catriona stood by the window. She wasn't going to sit either. 'Oh, *that's* why you're here,' said Lachlan, as if there could have been several dozen other reasons. 'I'm sorry you've had a wasted journey, then.'

'You mean you refuse?' Simon asked him.

'You could say that.' Lachlan looked across at Catriona, who was standing very still. 'Why don't you sit down, Catriona?'

'No, thanks.'

'As you wish, of course,' he nodded pleasantly.

'Let me get this straight, Mr Erskine,' said Simon. 'You are acting as agent on Crannich for the estate agents who have the property for sale, and yet you refuse me permission to view?'

'Yes,' Lachlan nodded.

'I can find out who the agents are,' said Simon.

'Oh, I'm sure you can. I'll save you the trouble. They're Messrs Peabody and Mackintosh, of Inverness.' He added, in almost kindly tones, 'They're in the phone book.'

Simon had gone slightly pale. It seemed, for the moment, as if he didn't know what to do, and Catriona said, because she couldn't bear it: 'Why won't you give us the keys?'

Lachlan's mouth curved slightly. 'I would have thought it obvious. I told you my feelings this morning. Now, if that's all you've come to say——'

'But it isn't,' Simon cut in. 'Not by a hell of a long way. First, I'm going to phone the agents on Monday and tell them just how obstructive you are——'

'You do that.' Lachlan nodded as if it seemed a good idea.

'And second, I'm going to contact Robert Bruce and let *him* know you're impersonating him—there are laws about that kind of thing, you know—and third, I never thought I'd meet someone as pathetic as you who can kid old people that you're someone important. My God, I'll make sure you're the laughing stock of London when you get back!'

'What *do* you mean?' asked Lachlan. His face had gone very serious, no traces of amusement there now. He seemed to have gone paler too, although that could have been a trick of the light. Catriona was rooted to the spot. She couldn't have spoken if she had wanted to. She felt sick inside, and empty. She wanted to leave, not to have to see Lachlan humiliated, as he was going to be, even if she did loathe him. No one deserved what Simon intended. She almost wanted to warn him——

Simon's mouth curled in contempt. 'What I said. You are *pathetic*. You really had Catriona's grandparents believing your little story. Couldn't you have picked a lesser name, if you *had* to assume an air of grandeur? Someone less known? You might just have got away with——'

'I'm not trying to get away with anything,' Lachlan cut in.

'Oh! You mean you *are* Robert Bruce?' drawled Simon with heavy sarcasm. 'Of *course*, I should have known!' He smiled. 'You're not Napoleon as well in your spare time, are you—as well as estate agent?'

'No. I have only the one pen name,' Lachlan said pleasantly. 'And if I chose to wipe that smile off your face I could do so in one minute. But I think I'll let you go on. I'm sure Catriona will find it entertaining.' He looked across at her. 'You need entertainment, don't you? Stay and listen—you'll see your precious friend go green very soon.' He glanced briefly at Simon. 'Carry on, I'm listening.'

'You're mad!' Simon's temper was rising. She could see it in the flush of colour high in his cheeks, by the way his hands clenched into fists at his side.

'No, I'm not. Perhaps you are. You think you're somebody important. You think you can come here and lay the law down, and insult me in my own home, and if there weren't a woman here I'd have thrown you out bodily by now——'

'Don't let Catriona's presence stop you trying,' Simon blazed. She saw the muscles tense in his shoulders, saw his stance, that of the boxer waiting for the bell.

'Don't be a bloody fool, man,' said Lachlan, as if suddenly weary of a game. 'Just get out and leave me in peace.'

'It's you who's the bloody fool!' Simon almost shouted the words. 'No one gets away with what you're trying to, with me—my God, you'll be sorry!'

'For what?' Lachlan advanced on him, and his face was dark with anger. 'For refusing you the keys? You can whistle for those, my friend—or for not giving a damn because you don't believe I write plays?' He laughed in Simon's face. 'Who the *hell* do you think *you* are, little man?'

Simon exploded. Catriona screamed as he launched himself on Lachlan, and ducked back out of the way. 'Stop it, stop it!' she cried, but it was too late. Trembling, she stood behind the settee and Simon crashed down on to it as if poleaxed. He was knocked out. Lachlan looked at her, his face harder than anything she had ever seen, and strode towards her. For one dreadful heart-stopping second she thought he was going to strike her, punch her as he had Simon, and she backed against the window, eyes wide with terror. He could kill her with one blow.

He caught her hand, and she felt the room spin round, and whispered, 'Please—don't hit me——'

'You fool!' he grated, voice harsh and deep. 'Do you think I could strike a woman?' He pulled her. 'Come with me.'

She stumbled round the settee, unable to do otherwise, for his grip was like steel, and he went across the room with her and opened a door to the back. There was a bed in the room—he was going to rape her—she felt her legs going from beneath her, then, finding strength from somewhere, she leaned down, bit his hand, and began to struggle to free herself from the nightmare.

'You bitch!' he muttered, and let her hand go. 'You stupid fool, did you think I was going to attack you? I'm not one of your London friends.' He stood and looked down at her, a man of steel, tough, tougher than she had remembered, and hard, and implacable. 'Just look,' he pointed. By the window was a desk, and a typewriter. He switched on the light and said to her, 'Go over to the desk—now.'

If she refused, he would very probably drag her over, or carry her, and she didn't want him to touch her again. Shivering, frightened, she walked over on unsteady legs and he followed her, and opened a drawer in the desk, picked out a bundle of papers and flung it on the desk. There was a letter attached to it by a paper clip. Lachlan lifted it off and put it in her hand. 'Read it,' he commanded, 'and tell me what it says.'

It was from a famous publisher of plays. She read, silently: 'Dear Lachlan, this could be the best yet. We've already been approached by a backer with a view to staging it, and we'll be in touch. As we are unable to contact you by phone since you moved to Crannich, will you please ring us *any* time, reversing the charges, for a chat about it. This could make it four on the go at once for Robert Bruce——' She read no further. She looked at him and he plucked the letter from her hand and gave her a thin smile.

'Well?' he said softly.

'You are——'

'Oh yes, I am. And when your lover wakes up, you can tell him—if you want to. I don't give a damn either way.' He walked out, went over to Simon, who sat looking drunk and bewildered on the settee, and hauled him to his feet. 'Fresh air will do you good,' he said, and to Catriona: 'Open the door. You can take him home now.'

She obeyed, and Simon was bundled ingloriously out, still groggy, but on his feet. Lachlan stood in the doorway, and as Catriona put her arm round Simon she turned, as if drawn by an irresistible force, and looked at him.

'Tell him,' said Lachlan, 'he won't get those houses. Not ever. It will save him wasting his time.' He closed the door very quietly, and they were alone.

Catriona lay in bed that night, still shocked and numbed by all that had happened. It was only ten o'clock, but she had a thumping headache, and she felt as weak as if she were sickening for 'flu.

Simon had gone. He had simply packed his case when they had reached the house, told her he wasn't staying there any longer, and left, in his car, to drive to the ferry. It had been nine o'clock. She had then had to go in and tell her grandparents—to whom he had not even bothered to say goodbye—and explain.

Their reaction had been surprising, to say the least. Her grandmother had looked up from the knitting she was doing while she watched a Charlton Heston film, and said: 'Oh dear, still, I sensed it was too quiet here for him. And after he brought you all that way too!' She had nodded sadly and gone back to her knitting. Her grandfather had spared her a brief glance from the screen—it was, after all, an interesting fight scene at the time—and said:

'Ungrateful young bounder! And he seemed so interested in the vegetable patch!'

Catriona had walked quietly out, gone into the kitchen and made herself a cup of coffee, and sat there drinking it. It was almost as if Simon hadn't been there. They didn't care. They just didn't *care*.

She had gone in, asked if they'd mind if she had an early night, kissed them, and gone up to bed. She lay watching the moon through the window, and tears filled her eyes. She didn't love Simon, but she was hurt by his action. No one ever walked out on her. And it had all been because of Lachlan.

She heard the clock in the hall strike ten, and, as its notes died away there was a knocking at the front door. She heard the lounge door open, her grandfather's footsteps across the hall, the door opening, then his voice greeting someone. Could it be Simon, coming back? She ran to the door and opened it, peeping out over the banister. Then she went cold. Lachlan and her grandfather were walking into the lounge. They were laughing.

She put her hand to her mouth and ran back into her room. Laughing, like old friends—or like conspirators.

She lay huddled under the covers, feeling a sense of betrayal, as if the world were turning against her. Dear God, what was happening? She had needed a break, and she had come here in answer to a plea from her grandparents; Simon had brought her, because she didn't drive, and because he couldn't do enough for her. She had no illusions about why. Any man seen with her more than once was automatically a celebrity, and speculation in the gossip columns of the daily papers was rife. 'Is this Kate Forbes' new love?' they would blazon to the reading public. Simon enjoyed that. He enjoyed any publicity because he always ensured that his advertising agency got a mention. He used her, even though he loved her—in his way—and she allowed him to, because he was presentable, good company—or always had been, until today—and because her life was not as the public seemed to think. It was often lonely. Too many men were scared to approach someone as successful as Catriona. She was often lonely, or had been until she had met Simon. He knew everyone, everywhere—or almost. He hadn't known Robert Bruce. But he had introduced Catriona to a new, fast-living crowd, who had taken her to them as the celebrity she was, and she had found life totally different over the past months. Much more different and tiring. She was due to start rehearsals for a B.B.C. play in four weeks. She had told her agent she was having a week or so off, and had come up with Simon, intending a few early nights. This was her first, and you couldn't get much earlier than nine-fifteen.

But if her grandparents were on Lachlan's side, then who was there left? She shivered. She had never felt so alone for a long time. Suddenly the wonderful, glittering world of acting seemed very hollow indeed. They had always been like an anchor, well in the background, but always there in the shifting fortunes of her meteoric rise to success. Perhaps she should have come here more often when, dazzled by the tinsel glitter, she had not always been able to see clearly who true friends were. Many actresses were envious of her, she knew that. They called her 'the Fire and Ice Maiden', not to her face, but behind her back. The fire of her hair and the ice of her heart, because it was well known that she didn't sleep around, as so many did. It wasn't for want of trying on the part of the men in her life. She had simply never met a man with whom she wanted to make love, not even Simon. Whether he implied that they were having an affair to his friends she neither knew nor cared. She knew the truth, and that was all that counted.

She also knew the deeper truth, one she had hidden well. There had been one man, once, whom she had thought she loved, and that man had rejected her. She had been very young, but had never forgotten, or forgiven. She could not bear to think about it even now, and had suppressed it until it had become buried in her subconscious. He would never know what he had done. She turned her head restlessly on the pillow. He would never know, because Catriona Forbes, alias Kate Forbes, much sought after actress, would never tell him, and only she knew the secret.

There was a knock at her door, she called listlessly: 'Come in,' and he walked in. Lachlan Erskine walked in, as though he knew whom she had been thinking about.

Catriona gasped. 'Go away!' she exclaimed.

'May I switch on the light?' he asked.

'No. Get out!'

He walked over and sat on the bed. 'Your grandparents gave me permission to come up and see you,' he said.

'Did they? How kind. How very kind,' she breathed. 'You got rid of Simon, are you going to get rid of them as well?'

'Not exactly,' he said. There was something in his tone ...

She sat up; she was at too much of a disadvantage under the covers. She snatched her dressing gown from behind him and draped it round her shoulders. 'Will you get off my bed?' she said icily.

He stood up and she pulled the light cord, and could see him clearly now. He picked up a chair and put it beside the bed, then sat down facing the back, arms straddling the wooden top. 'That's a relief anyway,' he said. 'I hope he's gone for good.'

'He'll be back,' she answered. 'What have you come to say? Please say it and go. I don't entertain men in my bedroom and I particularly don't want *you* here—or is your skin so thick that you're not aware of it?'

'I'm well aware of it,' he said. 'You're not an actress for nothing, Catriona. I'm sure you're brilliant at your job—and I do read the reviews—although I'm sure Meredith thought I couldn't even read.' He smiled. 'Did you tell him?'

'I thought you weren't interested whether he knew or not,' she said.

'I'm not really. I don't have to impress a pompous idiot like him——'

'But *you* told *me*,' she cut in. 'Don't tell me the great Robert Lachlan Bruce Erskine wants to impress *me*?' She laughed scornfully.

'Nor you either.' His glance was very hard, the grey eyes the colour of pebbles at the bottom of a pool. 'But I had a reason to let you know.'

'Tell me—then go.'

'Very well, I will. You might need time to adjust to it.'

'No, I won't. Just say, then leave. Nothing you can tell me would surprise me now.'

'You might be wrong there,' he commented, and his mouth moved slightly as if he hadn't decided whether to smile or not. He looked at her. 'I want your help,' he said.

Her eyes blazed. 'Whatever it is, the answer's no. I wouldn't help you if you were dying of thirst and I had a bottle of water!'

'Charming,' he murmured. 'The fire's blazing again, I see. Is it equally true about the ice?'

Catriona went very still. 'What do you mean?' she whispered through lips that scarcely moved.

'You must know what they call you.' He smiled. 'The Fire and Ice Maiden.'

'I do know. So?'

'Are you? All ice from the neck down?'

'Get out! Get *out* of *my* room!'

'I haven't finished yet.'

'Well, I *have*.' She put the dressing gown on, a black silk kimono, and jumped out of bed, too incensed to care that both nightdress and kimono were thin affairs, figure-hugging, emphasising her voluptuous curves.

She opened the door, but Lachlan remained seated. 'Short of throwing me out,' he remarked, 'there's not a lot you can do to make me leave. And I don't think you're strong enough, do you?'

'Oh, you've proved how tough you are, Lachlan,'

she spat. 'I'm sure you're proud of yourself. You always were a quick-tempered brute, weren't you? And you've not changed a bit.' She went over to him and gave him a hard slap across his face. 'How do you like *that*?' she breathed. He stood up then, pulled the chair aside, stepped forward, and took hold of both her arms.

'You shouldn't have done that,' he said, as the mark blazed on his cheek, then began to fade. 'You really shouldn't.' His eyes were narrowed and he looked even more dangerous than he had with Simon. 'Because you may regret it.'

'How?' She stared at him defiantly. He had said that he didn't hit women, and whatever else he was, she believed that.

'You'll see. Sit down.'

'No, damn you, I won't!'

He pushed her to the bed, and against it, until she was forced to sit. Then he stood in front of her, looking down at her. She pulled the edges of her kimono together, icily dignified.

'Now I'll tell you,' he said. 'I'm writing a new play. It's going badly—and I need your help.' As she looked up to spit fire at him again, he crouched down before her and raised a warning finger. 'Be quiet and listen,' he ordered. 'My patience is wearing thin. I want you to come with me to a little island called Farra, near here, and there we'll stay for a few days, while you help me go over the parts I need help on—act them out if you like—and you'll be able to do it, because it's about a successful actress who wearies of the burden of fame and escapes to a quiet place, to be alone, and to sort herself out——'

'I've heard enough!' Catriona jumped to her feet and looked down at him. Lachlan stood up slowly, and then she had to look up instead. 'You *are* crazy! *Me* come with *you* to an island? Hah! I wouldn't cross a road with you!'

'You'll come with me because you don't have any choice,' he told her. 'Because if you don't, your grandparents will have no home.'

Each word fell upon her ears with a strange bell-like clarity. She went very still, as a memory of an exchanged look, between her grandparents at dinner, came to her. Her grandfather had been talking about the house getting too much for them —and her grandmother had given him a warning shake of the head, and then changed the subject.

Icy cold, feeling almost lightheaded, she asked: 'What do you mean?'

'Haven't they told you? No, I can see they haven't. It's quite simple, Catriona. They sold me this house three months ago. It's too big and too old for them to maintain any more, and they're old themselves—so I bought it, but I said they can live here as long as they want. It's large enough to be split up, so they would have their own living quarters, more comfortable, maintained and heated by me—only, if you refuse what I ask, I shall turn them out. Is that clear enough for you to understand?'

She thought she would faint. This couldn't be real, it was some dreadful nightmare. She felt the

blood drain from her face, and sat down again.
'You—you wouldn't—you couldn't do it?' she said
tonelessly.

'I could, and I will. And if I do, they would have
to leave the island, for those other houses are mine
—which fact I didn't bother to tell Meredith. I
bought them too. So where would they go? London
—with you?'

'Dear God—you'd turn them out, just like that?'

'Yes. But if you come with me, do as I ask, it's
theirs for their lifetime. The responsibility is yours,
Catriona. What is it to be?'

'How do I know you would keep your word?' she
whispered.

'You would have it in writing, witnessed by a
lawyer. We'll go to Inverness on Monday.'

'And then?'

'And then we go to Farra, stay in the hotel there,
and I write my play—with you.'

She closed her eyes. 'You give me no choice,' she
said. 'It's—blackmail!'

'That's a strong word. Let's say it's an agree-
ment.' Lachlan walked away from her, towards the
door. 'I'll go and tell them the news—that you've
agreed to help me type out my play. That's all they
need to know.'

'Don't they know of your threat?'

He smiled. 'Dear me, no. I wouldn't want to
upset them. Nor would you.' He paused in the
doorway. 'Goodnight, Catriona. Sleep well.'

CHAPTER THREE

It was Monday morning. A dark blue Volvo stood outside the front door and Lachlan was opening the trunk. Mary Forbes smiled at Catriona. 'Such fun,' she said. 'You'll phone us before you get the boat to Farra? Lachlan tells me the phones there are very unreliable.'

'I promise.' Catriona hugged her. 'I just don't understand how you two can be so well—I thought, when I got your letter to come up, and phoned you about it, that you were neither of you feeling well.'

'Ach, it's just old age, that's all. We're fine, truly —we just wanted to see you.'

'But I'm leaving——' she began.

'Aye, with Lachlan, and only for a few days, he tells us. It'll give us time to do all our little jobs while you're away, then, when you come back, why, we'll have a *ceilidh*, with all the villagers, and I'll bake for it—— Oh,' she chuckled, 'it'll be like the old days!' She kissed Catriona. 'Off you go. Lachlan's a fine man, I'm sure he won't make you work hard.'

He's a blackmailer, thought Catriona, and the worst kind, and I hate him. Even if I didn't before, I do now. Her grandfather came into the hall from the kitchen just as Lachlan knocked at the door and her grandmother opened it. 'Here you are,' he said, pushing a large cardboard box into Catriona's arms. 'Some freshly picked vegetables for you.'

Lachlan had entered. He took the box from her and grinned at Mrs Forbes. 'Thanks,' he said.

'But we're going to a hotel,' said Catriona.

'So we are. Never mind, we'll hand these over— they might knock something off our bill, who knows?' He smiled at Mrs Forbes. 'You don't mind me borrowing Catriona for a few days, do you?' he asked.

'Not at all. You've been so kind to us, Lachlan.' She squeezed his arm. 'Just you get a good play written now, you hear?'

'I will.' He bent to kiss her cheek. Catriona watched, her heart like stone, her face bearing a bright happy smile. 'We'd better be off. I want to stop off in Inverness for a half hour, and then we've a boat to take. We'll see you soon!'

Catriona kissed her grandfather and followed Lachlan down the steps to the waiting car. As they drove away, still waving, she said: 'I hope you're satisfied.'

'I am. Why don't you relax? Two or three days' work, and a home for life for your grandparents. It's not much to ask.'

'It is—from you.'

He didn't answer. He was driving down the bumpy path to the village, and she could see the flat-bottomed ferry at the end of the road, to take

them on the half-mile journey to the mainland.
Then Inverness, and then·Farra, where she would
stay in a hotel with him. A thought struck her. 'I
trust we have separate rooms at this place we're
going?' she said.

Lachlan didn't even look at her. He was negoti-
ating the last steep curve before driving on to the
Ferry. 'Of course,' he said. 'What did you expect?'

'From you? God knows.' She watched as he
neared the boat, and old Finlay waved them on.
Catriona felt dry and empty. She had eaten nothing
at breakfast, drunk only a cup of tea, and she
wished she had never come back to Crannich. But
it was too late for that now. She was here, and with
him, and the next two days were going to be hell.

She thought she had had all the shocks she was
going to have. She hadn't imagined there could be
any more. But she was wrong, and she found out
how wrong when they reached the tiny village in
Wester Ross from where they were to take the boat
to Farra. She stood by the harbour as Lachlan
unloaded the luggage from the car trunk. The
village was tiny, there were no people about, only a
few inquisitive gulls, and four or five boats bobbing
gently in the water. The telephone kiosk from which
she had just rung her grandparents was over the
road.

'Do the MacBrayne's boats go from here?' she
asked.

'No.'

'Then how——' exasperated, she turned to him. 'How on earth do we get there?' she asked. He pointed. She looked at a large fishing boat with outboard motor, tied up to a post. 'That?' she exclaimed. 'We're going in *that*?'

'It's only a twenty-minute journey.' He carried their three cases down the stone steps and put them in the centre of the boat, which rocked, then settled. He came back, picked up the cardboard box of vegetables, handed it to her, and lifted a second box, after checking the trunk was locked. 'Let's go,' he said.

Catriona looked around as if seeking help. An old woman appeared in a cottage doorway and gave her a toothless smile, and she smiled back automatically. That was it. No one else about. She gritted her teeth and followed Lachlan down the steps. He lifted the cover off the outboard motor, checked it, and started it. 'Hold tight,' he said, and they curved round so that she was facing the shore, and she watched it recede, wondering what on earth she was doing here. It was mid-afternoon, and there was a faint mist out to sea, and, now that they were further from land, that too seemed to be becoming greyer, less clearly defined. I'm mad, she thought, and if anyone could see me now they'd wonder at my sanity—and if they knew *why* I was here, they'd know I was crazy. She watched him, hand on tiller, watching *her*. 'Is this your boat?' she asked.

'No, hired. Why?'

'I wondered. Don't they have regular runs to Farra?'

'Not any more.' It should have warned her, it really should. But it didn't. She leaned over and trailed her hand in the icy water.

'What's the name of the hotel?' she asked.

'The Garvain.'

'How big is it?'

'Only small.'

'Why are we going there? Why wouldn't you write your play on Crannich?'

'Because it's set on a deserted island, and Crannich's not.' There was an obvious question she should have asked then, but it didn't occur to her. Not then.

'You set one of your plays in an abandoned climber's shelter half way up a mountain,' she retorted smartly, 'but I don't suppose you *wrote* it there.'

'True. But I stayed in one for three nights absorbing the atmosphere.'

And still she didn't realise. Not until they landed on Farra some twenty minutes afterwards, and Lachlan jumped out and dragged the boat on to the shingle. Catriona too jumped out before he could offer her his hand. She was dressed in warm trousers, sweater and parka, and she wore rubber boots as he did, having changed in the car before they got out.

She stood on the empty beach and looked around her. The island was shrouded in mist, only the few cottages scattered nearby remaining fully visible. She couldn't see the tops of the hills; the mist rolled nearer even as she watched. A sense of desolation washed over her, and she shivered and turned to Lachlan, who was doing something to the outboard motor. 'It's even more deserted than that village,' she said, and her voice seemed to echo in the cold air.

'Yes, isn't it?' he answered, and began unloading. She took the cases one by one as he passed them to her and set them on the shingle. Then she knew what was wrong. There were no boats, not a single one. No nets hung out to dry either. A very strange sense of foreboding filled her, and she straightened up from the cases and looked at him as he passed her the box full of vegetables.

'There are no boats,' she said.

He looked around him, along the shore, slowly, thoughtfully, then turned back to her. 'No,' he agreed, 'there aren't.' He picked up the cases and said: 'This way. I'll come back for the others in a minute.'

She followed him. Their rubber boots scrunched grittily on the shingle, and they climbed steadily, then she saw the hotel. 'Hotel Garvain', it said, on a faded wooden board over the door, but there were no lights, and the door was closed. The place had a deserted look. The island had a deserted look, come to that. And then, belatedly, too late to do anything about it, she knew.

'This place—Farra—is empty, isn't it?' she asked him.

He nodded. 'Hmmm.'

'But you—you said——' She stopped. He hadn't actually said that Farra *wasn't* abandoned. He had given the impression that they would be staying at a hotel without adding that no one else would be there. 'I'm going,' she said.

'How?'

'I'm going in the boat. *You* can stay here and write your play and rot for all I care—I'm going home, I'm going to tell my grandparents what you've done, take them back with me to London and you can *go to hell*!' Her voice had been gradually rising as she spoke, and the last three words came out almost as a scream. Then she dumped the box down on the ground in front of the hotel and ran back towards the boat. She scrambled in, unzipped the cover from the outboard motor and pulled the string, once, twice, desperation giving her strength and speed as she prayed for it to work.

Lachlan walked slowly back towards the boat, not hurrying, sauntering almost. 'Damn, damn, *damn*!' Catriona swore under her breath. Something was wrong. He didn't seem concerned—he didn't seem——

'It won't work,' he told her, bending to pick up a suitcase and parcel. 'I removed a rather vital piece of the engine, you see.'

He stood there and looked at her, and Catriona crouched in the boat, a trembling bundle of concentrated fury, her eyes wide, face white, wishing she were strong enough to kill him.

He leaned forward and reached out his hand.

'Come on,' he said. 'A cup of tea will do you——'

'Don't touch me! Don't, *touch* me!' she burst out. 'I hate you!'

'That's a strong word. You don't, you know. After a hot meal and a seat by the fire, you'll calm down.'

'I damned well won't!' She jumped out of the boat and faced him. 'Of all the despicable things to do, this is the worst! You expect me to stay *here* with *you*—alone——'

'Only for a few days.' He stepped forward. 'Are you coming now, or do I have to carry you there?'

'I'm not going anywhere with you!'

'Right,' he said. 'We'll see, won't we?' And he picked her up and carried her, struggling and screaming, back to the hotel, pushed the door open, dumped her unceremoniously down on the floor, bolted the door, and walked over to a table. Catriona stood there and watched, listened as there was a click, a flare, and a lamp glowed warm and bright, filling the room with light.

They were in a small but wide hallway. A reception desk loomed darkly at the back. There were chairs at intervals, and in an old fireplace, a log fire was laid with paper and sticks, underneath. There was a high mantelshelf over the brick fireplace, with a bottle of whisky standing on it. Catriona looked around her, face tightening with anger.

'You expect me to stay here?' she demanded.

'Yes. This way. I'll show you the kitchen,' he

answered, and picked up the lamp. She followed because she had no choice, and because she didn't want to be left in darkness, and because, for the moment, she didn't know what else to do.

Lachlan led the way down a passage to the left, and into a large room with a cooker, and a table, and cupboards. He lit another lamp, placed one on the mantelpiece of the old-fashioned kitchen range, bent down and set a match to the laid fire, then went and pumped water into the kettle from a hand pump in the sink. There was a further 'plop' as the gas lighted, and he put the kettle on.

Shadows danced in the corners of the room as the light from the fire blazed up. There were two beakers and two plates on the draining board, a tea tin and a jar of coffee and one of powdered milk. It was all too—ready. A suspicion that had been growing since he had lit the first lamp in the hall was gnawing at her, and she voiced it. 'You've been here before and got this ready, haven't you?' she accused.

'I have.' He turned from the stove. 'Tea or coffee?'

'Coffee.' She sat down. 'When?' There was a sick dread inside her.

'Nearly a week ago.'

'When you knew—I'd be coming up?'

'Yes.'

'So this was all planned—before?'

'Of course. I don't do things on impulse.'

'But why—why?' she whispered.

'I've told you, I need your help.'

Catriona put her hand to her burning forehead. Who was mad? He or she? It was planned, like an inexorable fate—he had intended, a week ago, to bring her here, and now he had done so. He had intended Simon to leave Crannich, and he had. It was as though he had the power to make things happen. She felt herself shivering, very cold, and he made two cups of coffee, added powdered milk, and gave her one. 'I'll prepare a meal soon,' he said. 'You'll feel better and warmer—when you've eaten.'

She would never be warm again. The room was chilly, even though the fire was beginning to burn. She cupped the beaker in her hands, and that warmth was comforting, but not enough. 'Why me?' she asked.

'Why not? You're ideal. When you see the main character in the play, you'll know why. You'll find it an interesting experience, Catriona.'

'No, I won't. I hate the thought of being here with you!'

He sat down on the other chair. It was like coming into a ghost house, with everything ready. Two cups, two plates, two chairs—all waiting for them to arrive. 'Because you'd rather be in London with Simon and his friends?'

'Anything's better than this,' she said bitterly. She swallowed some of the hot strong coffee.

'No, it's not. This is the best place for you to be.'

'With you? A blackmailer? A liar?'

'I had to get you here somehow. Would you have come if I'd just asked?'

She didn't answer, she didn't need to. Lachlan smiled, with irony.

'So I did it my way.'

'And now you've got me here, do I have to fight you off every step of the way?'

'Is that how you regard men? As potential rapists? Is that the kind of crowd you mix with? That's what you thought when I took you into the back room at my house—is that what Simon and his crowd have done for you?'

She looked at him then. 'Why do you talk like this? You don't know anything about Simon.'

'Yes, I do. Far more than you think. And, I suspect, far more than you do yourself. Do you love him?'

'That's none of your business!'

'I just made it mine. Do you?' His voice was sharp.

'No. Satisfied?'

'Enough—for now. I'll give him credit for one thing. He does think quite a lot of you.'

'Well, thank *you*,' she retorted.

'At any rate, as much as he can think a lot of anyone except himself. Which is why it's not too late.'

'You're talking in riddles,' she said. 'I'm hungry. When are we going to eat?'

'I've switched the bottom oven on. We'll have pizza tonight—I brought two big ones loaded with cheese and tomato. There'll be enough. And to-morrow we'll divide the jobs equally.' He regarded her steadily across the table. 'After a few days here you'll be a different woman.'

'After a few days in your company I'll need to—what do you mean, after a *few* days? You said we were staying two.'

'Two might not be enough.'

Catriona went white with shock. It hit her with the force of a blow, as he stood up and walked out of the room, taking a lamp with him. When he returned he was carrying a box from which he took two cartons and opened them. He put the pizzas into the oven and closed the door.

'Oh, God,' she whispered. 'What are you doing?'

'Putting pizzas in the oven.'

'Not that! To me—why? Why?'

Lachlan came over, pulled her to her feet, and held her in his arms. 'I'm going to make you see yourself as you really are,' he said. 'And you might not like what you see—but it'll be you.'

You. You. You. The word echoed in her head, and she shook it, trying desperately to free herself. 'I don't know you,' she cried. 'I don't know you at all—you're like a stranger, a frightening stranger, and I can't bear it. Let me go—please, let me go!'

'No.' He shook her, and his voice was harsh and deep.

She looked up at him and whispered: 'You made them ask me to come, didn't you? There's nothing wrong with my grandparents at all. It was you.'

'Yes, it was me.' He gazed down at her face.

'What hold do you have over them?'

'None. They were concerned about you. I—suggested they write, that was all.'

'But you—you always get what you want,' she said. 'You told me that——' She shivered helplessly, and he held her head against his breast, and she felt the strong steady beat of his heart, but this wasn't frightening now, it was a safe place to be, a very safe, secure place. He moved slightly, and his hand was on her chin, tilting her face upwards. Then his lips came down on hers, in a long sweet kiss, with tenderness, and warmth, and a sensual awareness that took her by surprise and filled her with a heady response that both dismayed and excited her. She had been kissed many times, by many men, but there had been none like this. She was left weak and shaking when he released her, and she moved away, sanity returning, and put her hand to her lips, and her other hand on the table to steady her.

'You had no right to kiss me,' she said.

'Perhaps not, but you didn't stop me. I wanted to see what is was like to kiss a famous actress.'

'You write plays—you must have known many actresses.'

'I don't mix business with pleasure.'

She went very still. 'But this is—this is—business.'

'Not exactly.' Lachlan smiled. His eyes were shadowed and dark. 'Let's call it a rehearsal——'

'For what?' she asked breathlessly.

'For what is to come.'

She turned away. Her heart was pounding. 'And what is that?'

'I don't know yet. It's not written.'

'I don't understand you,' she said helplessly.

'You don't need to, not yet. Just wait. You will.'

'We're going to stay here, aren't we? Just stay here, you and me, for days and days, and it'll be like forever—and you're—you're going to make love to me, aren't you?'

Lachlan stood there looking at her, not answering, and she caught her breath at the expression on his face and went to him. 'Answer me!' she demanded.

'Is that what you want?'

'*No!*'

'Then we won't. I wouldn't force you. You should have realised that by now.'

'But you'll—you forced me here against my will,' she pointed out.

'That's different.'

'No, it's not. It's all part of a pattern, only I can't see it clearly, yet—you frighten me.'

'You have no need to be frightened, Catriona,' he assured her. 'Not of *me*.'

'Of whom, then? There's no one else here.'

'Simon.'

'He'll be back in London now.'

'Probably. And trying to find out as much as he can about me—and he'll be back, you can be sure of that.'

'And I'll return to London with him——' she began.

'Not if I have anything to do with it, you won't.' His face had gone harder again.

'You don't run my life!' she burst out.

'I didn't say I did.' He turned away, but she went after him and grabbed hold of his arm.

'I'm an actress—I have a job, remember? I'm committed to a part in a play soon.'

'Then the sooner we get *this* play done, the better.'

'*You're* the playwright, not me! Do you think I'm going to help you do your work for you?' she said angrily.

'In a way, yes.' He gave her a bleak hard look. 'Oh yes—in a way.'

She shivered. 'Then you'll be disappointed. I only speak words, not create them.'

'Then speak here—that's all I ask.'

'What do you mean?' she whispered.

'Don't you know? Just be yourself, talk about yourself.'

'To you? Tell you my innermost thoughts?'

'Something like that.'

'Like *hell* I will! You know nothing about me— and you never will——'

'I know far more about you than you imagine, Catriona,' he said softly.

His words had the ring of truth to them, and they were a shock. 'How can you?' she whispered.

'Only what's in the papers.'

'Not that.' He laughed softly. 'I never believe what I read in those—oh dear, no.' He looked at her, and there was something almost akin to pity in his glance. 'You're very unhappy, Catriona—and you need help.'

'I don't. I *don't*! How dare you say such *stupid* things!'

'I can because they're true, and you know it.' He grasped her upper arms and faced her, and he wasn't going to let her move away, not until he was finished, and she didn't want to hear his dreadful words—She tried to pull herself free, and it was useless, his grip was like steel.

'Let me go,' she begged, eyes bright with anger and tears. 'Let me go!'

'Not yet. Not for a while yet. You've got in with a dangerous crowd—and you don't know it yet, but you will, before I've finished. Oh yes, you will.'

Catriona felt the ground tilting, the room start to sway and swim round; she cried out something, she knew not what, and felt her pulses pound.

When she opened her eyes she was lying on top of a bed. It was a large bed, in a small room, and Lachlan was sitting on the edge of the bed, looking at her. 'You fainted,' he told her. 'You've eaten next to nothing today. You'll eat properly while we're here. This is a room next to the kitchen where the proprietor and his wife slept when the hotel was full. My room is next door. It's easier to keep these two rooms heated in cold weather now the electricity's off.' She saw a round pattern of light on the ceiling, and smelt the faint but familiar odour of paraffin. It brought back memories of childhood when there had been a Valor heater in the bedroom in winter. She sat up slightly, and saw a familiar tall round shape. The heater was in the centre of the room, and it had taken the chill off the air. 'There are four hot water bottles. You'll be warm and comfortable while you're here.' He stood up. 'The pizzas are ready. Are you coming out to eat?'

'Yes.' She sat up properly, and swung her feet over the side of the bed, to the floor.

'Good. Come on, then.'

She stood up. Lachlan made no attempt to help her, but watched her walk to the door. Catriona felt disjointed, disorientated. And she felt frightened. She had to humour him, because he was obviously mad, and she hoped she would have the strength to carry it off. He wanted her to talk about herself, that was what he had said, so she would. She would talk, and talk, if that was what he wanted. She sat down at the kitchen table and waited for him to start probing.

He didn't. He dished out the pizzas, handed her a freshly made cup of tea, and sat down. He told her about the island and its history, and why the people had left, and he made it interesting. His obvious gift for words painted the pictures brightly for her, and she ate without being aware that she was eating, and when she had finished he put a bowl of fresh fruit on the table, and a plate of cheese and biscuits, and she helped herself to those as well.

The dreadful scene of before might not have happened. Catriona began to wonder if she had imagined it. She listened, and she watched him as he began to tell her how he had started writing, and of the various misadventures that had dogged his first efforts, and he was like a different man. The hardness had gone. His face, in the warm light of the paraffin lamps, was softened, made almost gentle. He was very attractive, his features strong, almost beautiful, and for some reason he was exerting himself to be charming. It was such a contrast that she felt confused—but at the same time grateful. She was in his hands entirely. He had the power to make her stay on Farra a hell if he chose. She didn't want that. She wanted kindness and a rest from the stress of her life. She felt as if she wanted to sleep for days, and not wake up. She ached with the exhaustion that had built up gradually over a period of months, so gradually that she had scarcely been aware of the pressures. It had hit her, though, before she fainted, and she knew now why she had. It was because he had spoken the truth, and because it was too unbearable to hear she had blanked out her mind to it. But how did he know? That was one question remaining that she dared not ask.

CHAPTER FOUR

CATRIONA slept soundly on the hard but comfortable bed, one bottle at her feet, another at her waist. She slept so soundly that when she awoke she didn't know where she was, and lay for a moment or two trying to remember.

A watery sun slanted in through the dusty windows, and a gull flew past, crying harshly. Then she remembered. She was on the island of Farra with Lachlan Erskine, they were alone, and she was his virtual prisoner.

A tantalising scent of bacon drifted through the open door, and she heard whistling, the clatter of plates, a door closing somewhere, then silence.

She went to the window, which overlooked the yard at the back of the hotel, and looked out. Lachlan was filling a bucket with logs from a shed at the back of the cobbled yard, and an inquisitive gannet sat on the roof of it and watched him with beady eyes. She saw him walk back across the yard and into the kitchen, then the door closed. The gannet flew away, and she watched it go, its wings flapping gracefully until it was caught in a current of air and glided out of sight.

Catriona belted her warm dressing gown round her waist, put her slippers on, and went out along the short stone passage to the kitchen. Lachlan knelt by the fire, which was burning well, and laid on three more logs. Bacon sizzled in one pan, eggs and tomatoes in another. The smell was totally irresistible.

Lachlan looked up. 'Good morning,' he said. 'Are you hungry?'

'I'm starving,' she admitted. 'What time is it?'

'About ten. I let you sleep on. I've been up since seven. I'll show you around the hotel after we've eaten, get the feel of the place. Sit down, it's nearly ready.'

'I thought there was going to be a division of labour?'

'There is, but not at this moment. You need food first, then we'll get organised. Can you cook?'

'Yes.'

'Then we'll have fish for lunch. I was out and caught three mackerel.'

'And I'll cook them?'

'Yes.' He produced plates from the oven and put out bacon, egg, and tomatoes on them. Cut bread was on the table, as was butter and marmalade. 'Eat up,' he ordered.

Catriona ate everything that was on her plate, then had bread butter and marmalade. She drank her coffee black and sweet, and when at last she had finished that she sat back. 'That was good. I enjoyed it,' she said. 'When do we start work?'

'After we've seen round—and after you're dressed.' Lachlan got up and took the steaming kettle from the stove. 'Here's hot water for your wash.'

'Thank you.' She took it from him and went into the small bathroom next to her bedroom. The door of the room beyond that was open, and she could see his case by the neatly made bed. The part they were in was self-contained, like a flat at the back of the hotel. The bathroom was tiny, with old-fashioned fittings, and there was a folded towel beside his on the rail. The bath was a huge old one with a Calor gas heater near it. Catriona wondered if it worked. She liked one bath a day, whenever possible, but for now she would make do with a good wash. She felt that if she trod carefully he would stay pleasant. He was infinitely preferable like that to the other, harder stranger she had glimpsed.

When she was washed and dressed, and had made her bed, she went out to the kitchen, carrying the empty kettle. He sat at the table, writing in a large exercise book. 'Ready?' he asked.

'Yes.' She had tied her glorious red hair back with a yellow scarf, and she wore a matching sweater, and blue jeans and her slippers. Lachlan was dressed in jeans and a black polo-necked sweater—and rubber boots.

He looked at her footwear. 'Better change those,' he said.

'Are we going out?'

He nodded. 'A walk round the island. It's not a large one.'

She didn't argue, as she might have done only yesterday. She took off the slippers and donned her rubber boots. He held her warm parka out to her and she put that on as well. When they went out into the yard she felt the cold air on her face. 'Aren't you wearing a coat?' she asked.

'No, it doesn't bother me.' There was a gate at the side of the shed; Lachlan opened it and they walked towards the front of the hotel, down a narrow passage between it and the neighbouring cottage. He glanced at her. 'You're very quiet,' he commented.

'Wouldn't you be, if you were me?' she looked back at him. He smiled but said nothing, and they walked along the empty roadway, past the row of cottages, all abandoned and silent. It was eerie. Catriona had never been anywhere like this before, with not a soul living there. Behind the cottages the ground rose sharply into bleak rocky hillside with sturdy trees clinging for life to the precarious ground. Heather grew in clumps in the soil outside some of the cottages, and several gorse bushes and weeds.

The air was sharp and clean, slightly salty, and the breeze blew in from the sea, stinging her cheeks with invisible spray. Catriona wondered what was happening to her. She hadn't walked for years, not like this, not following an empty shoreline, wearing rubber boots and parka, with the breeze teasing her hair, and with a man she didn't like, and she thought she would hate it, but she didn't. They

had passed the cottages now; there was one shop at
the end, outside which stood a telephone kiosk.
The telephone had been taken out and there were
no wires leading to the telegraph pole standing
sentinel beside it. Lachlan went towards the shop
and opened the door, and she followed him inside.
The dusty shelves were empty, and a pile of yellow-
ing newspapers was the only item on the counter.
There was a faint lingering smell of paraffin and
soap powder in the dry air. Catriona looked around
her. 'How sad to see it all—dead, somehow, now,'
she said, and went over to look at the papers. The
dates were all of three years previously, long-
forgotten headlines, meaningless, history.

'Yes, it is. But that's life for you, and progress.
Everything changes.' Lachlan went behind the
counter and bent down. When he stood up, he put
something on the counter, something small and
bright. It was a red button. She picked it up.

'I wonder what that was doing there?' she said.

'Waiting for us to find it,' he said drily, and she
put it in her pocket, she didn't know why, and they
walked out again. Along, up a rough track, climb-
ing slightly and going away from the shore. They
walked, and neither spoke until they reached the
highest point of the island and there they stopped
to look out to sea. Catriona sat down on a flat rock.
The land swept away and down to the cottages,
only the roofs of which were visible. Gulls wheeled
in the sky, the sea stretched away to the distant
coastline of the mainland, and far out at sea a

small fishing boat moved slowly, near the horizon.

Something was changing. She didn't know what it was, or why, but she was coming to an acceptance of her role there, and, in a strange way, an acceptance of the man who stood nearby, watching the ship. He stood quite still, apparently lost in thought, for it was as though he had gone away from her, as if he were not aware that she was there.

Straight and tall and powerful, he stood there and surveyed the calm sea, like a conqueror laying claim to his land. Catriona blinked. Now she was getting fanciful. Lachlan was the one with the dreams that he transmitted to words, not her. He made the words for people to say, to conjure up images in the minds of audiences, and he did it well.

She had been to two of his plays—unaware that he was the author—and they had been vivid experiences, the kind that left the watchers enriched for having witnessed something special. One of the plays had been light, a comedy about two married couples in suburbia, their problems and the complications that ensued when an old flame of one of the husbands came to live nearby. But the other she had seen had been very different, and very moving. The impact had lasted for a long time, and she still remembered the effect it had had on her, even now. The shattering story of a man haunted by his past who has to come to terms with what he had done many years before, a crime for which he had never been caught, and which has preyed on him ever since. The play had gradually built to a nail-biting climax—and in the theatre, as it neared the end, not a sound could be heard, save the words of the two principal actors. No one coughed, or fidgeted, or whispered—but the tension, gathered in the two hours of the action, had filled every person in the audience. As the curtain fell, there was complete and utter silence for several heart-stopping seconds, then the whole place had erupted with deafening applause. That went on, and on, and on ...

She felt a tremor run through her at the memories. This man had written that play. This man who had blackmailed her here, who knew all about Simon—far more than she herself, if he was to be believed, and who was going to use her, and who was quite ruthless—had brought her here.

He had changed in the years since he had been away, physically and obviously mentally. It had been ten years when she had last seen him, she fifteen, he twenty-two, and she would never forget his going. She would never forget that day when she had seen him step on to the ferry, holding one small suitcase. She had been watching from the hillside, hidden by the trees, and she had wanted to die. He hadn't looked back. He had been thinner then, as tall as now, but not mature.

Yet when she had seen him with Simon, in the woods, when he had stepped out from behind the tree with his shattering words, it had been as though time itself had rolled back. In him at that moment she had glimpsed the young man, just for an instant, the one who had gone away and never looked back.

She wondered if he remembered. He had said something to her, in the woods, three days ago— he had said: 'I should have known you'd bring trouble when you returned.' The echo of his words rang in her ears and she caught her breath. She had forgotten them, because the fight with Simon afterwards put them out of her mind. They had been cruel, but Lachlan had meant them, and if he had wanted to hurt her he had succeeded. She looked up at him, and he had turned, and was watching her steadily, silently. So this was why he had brought her here. For revenge.

She stood up slowly. 'I want to go back,' she said. She wasn't going to faint again, or behave stupidly. That was over now. She was no longer the gauche fifteen-year-old who had thought she loved him, but a mature woman. He couldn't kill her. He could—he was physically capable, but he wouldn't. That wouldn't be his way. It would be something more subtle, and perhaps it had already begun.

'Then we'll go,' he said. 'You can see round the hotel and tell me what you think of the atmosphere there.'

'Can't you decide for yourself?'

'Yes. It would be interesting to hear your opinions, though.'

She would give him some, then, if that was what

he wanted. She was going to play the best role of her acting career, and it was starting now. The curtain was going up on Act One very shortly, but first the scene had to be set, the costumes and make-up had to be just right.

'Just a minute,' she said as they went into the kitchen. 'I want to go and change before looking round.'

'I'll put the kettle on, then.'

'Thanks. I'd love a coffee.' She sailed out, went into her bedroom and took out her make-up case. She simply hadn't bothered that morning, but she couldn't act without make-up, it was part of her *persona*, and it would help. She left the figure-hugging jeans on, but took off the yellow sweater and found instead a jade green silk tunic that matched her eyes. It was long, hip-length, with full sleeves and low V-neck. She loosed her hair and let it fall in soft waves round her face after making up lightly and skilfully to make herself look paler, more fragile; the merest whisper of lipstick, and she was ready. She took a deep breath and felt the butterflies she always felt just before filming began for TV plays. The only difference was, this time she had no script. The words would be her own.

She took a last look at herself in the dressing table mirror. Her skin was flawless, her face softly rounded, and she had emphasised her classic cheek-bones with blusher and white shadow. Her lips were full and delicately curved, feminine, and the pale pink lipstick enhanced without exaggerating.

She needed little eye make-up. Her lashes were naturally thick and dark, and her eyebrows were well shaped—due to careful plucking every week. But she had used a little green eye-shadow, not enough to be obvious, just a subtle highlight for the colour of her eyes.

She was satisfied, and walked into the kitchen to see him writing again. Two beakers stood on the table.

'Thank you,' she said. 'Is this the play you're writing now?'

Lachlan looked up then, and she saw the quick reaction on his face before he concealed it. He knew there was a difference all right—but he wasn't sure what it was, and she knew he wouldn't comment. 'Yes,' he answered. 'Just notes, you know.'

'I see. You'll take it round with us?'

'No, that's not necessary.'

She sat down at the table and picked up the beaker, each movement studied, as she would do it on set. The only difference was, no cameras.

'I can tell you now,' she said, 'even before we look round. The atmosphere here is quite eerie. I felt it particularly as we walked round the island today. It's got an almost haunted air to it. I don't think I'd like to be here alone.'

'Could you imagine you were?'

She laughed. It was more of a low throaty chuckle. 'You want me to try?'

'Yes.'

'But you don't need me to help you get under the skin of your characters, surely?'

'It will give added depth if I get your own reaction.'

'Then of course—if that's what you want.' She looked round the room, slowly, languorously, as if playing to an unseen camera. 'Why don't you let me wander round on my own?'

'Of course.'

'Surely the play doesn't only have one character in it?' she queried.

'No. But she's alone at first, for a few days—or thinks she is.'

Catriona caught her breath. 'What do you mean?'

'She comes to this island, as I've told you, a world-weary actress, seeking peace. It's a place she remembers from childhood. She hires a boat—as we did—comes to the hotel she stayed at, happily, years before, and she's going to sort herself out, one way or another.'

'You mean—if she doesn't find the peace she seeks——'

'She'll kill herself. Yes.'

'My God!' She could almost see it. Remembering the sense of desolation when she arrived, the looking along that deserted shore—with no boats—that had been eerie. She told him of that, and watched him making notes as she spoke, then he looked up.

'You see? You've got it already—that's fine!'

'But you knew—you must have known this is how I would feel.'

'You're a woman,' he explained. 'Your reactions are subtly different from a man's.'

'But you've written about women before.'

'Never like this.'

Catriona traced a pattern on the table with her finger. 'You said—she *thought* she was alone.'

'Yes. She isn't. There's someone else already here.'

'A man?'

'Yes. Can you guess what kind of man?'

She thought about it, picturing the scene, almost like a stage set. It wouldn't be anyone ordinary—it would be someone with his own motive for going to a deserted place. 'A—criminal? Someone on the run?'

'Not quite. But you're getting the idea. Not a criminal exactly.'

She was, despite herself, intrigued. She had never thought she would be, but she wanted to know. She shook her head.

'I give in.'

'The man is a seaman who has defected from a Russian trawler. He has swum to the island to escape, and been living rough there for weeks when she arrives. He is a man totally unlike her, from a different background and race, and a different culture——' Catriona was listening intently, forgetting about her own rôle.

'He thinks, obviously, that it's some kind of

trap. He watches her. The audience will be aware of him watching her—and the tension will build up from there. I gave you the impression it's a stage play. It's not. I'm writing this for television.'

'Yes, yes,' she waved her hand impatiently. 'Go on.'

'That's it, so far. Obviously, she's brought enough food for herself for a week. After that she either goes back to rejoin the world, or——' Lachlan paused.

She breathed deeply. 'And?'

'It's the reaction they trigger off in each other, he seeking freedom of one kind, she of another. He wants to live, she doesn't care whether she lives or dies.'

'What happens in the end?'

He smiled slightly. 'If I knew, we wouldn't be here.'

She shivered, then stood up. 'Let me wander round, now while all you've told me is fresh in my mind. I promise, I'll think myself into the part, and tell you all I see.' She finished her coffee, walked away from him towards the door. There she paused. 'What name have you given to her?' she asked.

'I haven't decided.'

'She's got to have a name. I can identify more if I know.'

'Then tell me one.'

'No, it's your play, your character.'

He stood up and walked over to her. 'Catriona?'

he said softly.

'No! It's not me!'

'It can be. *Be* her—believe yourself to be her.'

'I can't.' She stood holding the door frame and stared at him, her eyes wide.

'It would be the rôle of your life.'

'No.' She shook her head.

'Scared?' he taunted.

She moved slightly away. 'No, it's—not that.'

'Then what is it?'

She shook her head. 'I don't—know.'

'Try it,' he said, and his eyes held a strange darkness, a strength that reached out to her. Her heart beat rapidly. She felt as if she were drowning.

'I'll try,' she said slowly, and ran her tongue along her dry lips

'Good.' He walked away, satisfied. 'Off you go.'

Catriona went down the narrow passage and opened the door to the front part of the hotel. She went into the entrance hall and stood there for a few minutes, taking it all in, thinking herself into the part. When she was satisfied, she went slowly up the stairs.

It was an hour before she returned to the kitchen. Lachlan had a tape recorder on the table, and he was standing by the back door, which was open, letting in the cool air. He turned as she walked slowly into the kitchen, and saw her face. He walked quickly towards her and took her arm.

'Sit down,' he said.

Catriona looked at him and felt as if she were coming back from a long way away.

'How did it go?' he asked.

She gave him a very faint smile. She felt as she did after a gruelling performance, drained of energy, totally exhausted. 'I'd like a drink,' she said.

'Coffee? Something stronger?'

'Something stronger.' She watched him produce the bottle of whisky and pour some into a beaker.

'No glasses, sorry.' He handed it to her.

'Aren't you having any?'

'No. Not when I'm working I don't.'

It was work to him. It was a play; his job, just as acting was hers. Catriona swallowed some of the mellow malt whisky, then she looked at him, and he switched on the tape recorder and held his pen poised.

She began to speak, telling him, right from the beginning, her feelings and emotions as she had gone into each room of the hotel, aware as she did so that she spoke as the Catriona of the play, the frightened unhappy woman who had run away from the world.

The strangest thing had happened in one room. She had deliberately imagined that someone was watching her—and her own reaction had been scary to her. She had actually tasted real fear, the heart-pounding fear of someone who, thinking herself to be entirely alone, miles away from any human beings, is suddenly aware of someone—or something else—not far away. Of being watched. She described this to him—and he stopped writing. He simply stopped, and looked at her, and as she finished he muttered: 'My God! That's *it*!'

It was like being jerked on a string. 'What is?' she said.

'Your reaction—the fear, the feeling of wanting to go and hide, lock yourself away, safe——'

'But don't you see? I imagined it—and that was how it took me.'

'Yes, but it never occurred to *me* that that was how you would feel.'

'I don't understand,' she said. 'What would your reaction have been?'

'Mine? To find some sort of weapon and go and find whatever—whoever—it was.'

She gave a disbelieving laugh. 'Come off it!'

Lachlan looked at her blankly. 'That's what a man would do.'

She realised—and it had been growing on her for some minutes—that they were talking together like two colleagues, not like the enemies they were. The conversation was on a different level from anything that had been before. It was, of course, what she wanted, but it was quite disturbing in a way.

Lachlan switched the tape recorder off. 'That's enough for now.' Catriona tried to relax, but she couldn't. She was too tense, with the memory of living a part. She stood up and went to the door, opened it and looked out. The sun had vanished. It was noon, but it had become, quite suddenly, like dusk. The mist was rolling down from the hills, which were obscured, and the yard was already grey and damp-looking.

She whirled back and slammed the door. 'I don't like it here,' she said. 'Look outside—it's like night, yet it's midday.'

'It's only mist.' He glanced at the window. 'It's autumn. What do you expect? You have them on Crannich too.'

'It's different there,' she said. 'There are people. Here, it's just us—or is it?' She put her hand to her head. 'That damned play of yours has got me jumpy.' She shivered, suddenly chilled, and looked across to see the fire burning merrily. 'It's gone colder.' She rubbed her arms. 'I'm—cold.'

'Put a sweater on.'

'Is that all you can say? Put a sweater on? My God, what are you, a man or a machine?' The reaction had caught her strongly. She wanted to throw something at him, to hurt him. He had sat there watching her as though she were some laboratory guinea-pig, listening, taping, writing—she felt her face burn with anger. 'Damn your play!'

'Calm down.' He stood up and walked over to where she stood by the door. Lachlan Erskine, fiery-tempered Lachlan, was being calm and reasoning, as though she were a wilful child to be humoured. 'You'll feel better when you've eaten.'

'I don't want any food. I'm not hungry,' she snapped. 'Is that your cure for everything—food? The psychiatrists would have a few theories about *that*!' She glared at him, and he began to laugh.

'Don't laugh at *me*!' she stormed.

'Don't say ridiculous things and I won't,' he

grinned.

'Simon was right about you,' she said. 'He said you were a thug, and you are!'

'A moment ago I was a machine. And Simon Meredith's opinions don't do much for me. I'd be more worried if I thought he liked me.'

'Oh, shut up!' she retorted. 'You think you know it all, don't you?'

'Enough. More than you, apparently.'

'You've been hinting all along that you know him. Well, how come *he* didn't know *you?*' she demanded, glaring.

'Because he goes around making the maximum amount of fuss. He knows everyone—or thinks he does. I get on with what I have to do as quietly as possible.'

'Ha!'

'As quietly as possible,' he repeated, 'which means that while I find out things about loud-mouths like Meredith, no one finds anything out about *me*—unless I want them to know.'

'You make yourself sound like Sherlock Holmes!'

'I don't *make* myself sound like anything— except me.' He stood there and looked at her, big, dark, powerful, and his voice had a relentless grating to it. She would never win an argument with him, because he had an answer for everything she said. She had never encountered anybody like him before. He didn't fit into the conventional mould of the successful man. He seemed not to give a damn about appearances. He wrote under an assumed name, and was never photographed. He owned houses on Crannich, he wrote brilliant plays, and he was ruthless. He had wanted her here and she had been given no choice about coming. He had been here before and prepared it, so confident was he that he would succeed. So why was she bothering to even try and argue? It would be so much easier to agree with everything he said. She had decided that before. Why, she wondered, have I forgotten what I resolved to do so quickly?

She turned away. 'Of course. You're right,' she said. 'We'll eat. I'll prepare lunch if you'll show me where the fish are. And afterwards we'll talk and you can record what I say. That's what you want, isn't it? A docile woman doing your bidding?' She held out her hands in a gesture of surrender. 'All right, you've got one. I know when I'm beaten.' She walked back to the table, and there was defeat and submission in every line. He'd get what he wanted—and he would never know it was an act.

She was whirled round, held by one arm, and he gave her a wry smile. 'Beautiful,' he said. 'Perfect! You'd win an Oscar for that little performance if the cameras had been recording it. Which play was it you did that brave little walk in——' he got no further. Catriona, incensed, lashed out at him wildly. The next second she was helpless.

CHAPTER FIVE

'THE submissive little woman bit didn't last long, did it?' he grated. 'I've told you before not to hit me. I don't like being slapped—not when I can't slap back!'

'Go to hell!' Catriona knew better than to try and struggle free this time. She looked up at him defiantly, eyes blazing.

'I'll take you with me if I do.' He laughed softly, not hiding the mockery in his face.

'I wish I was a man,' she whispered. 'And stronger than you!'

'Simon thought that—it didn't get him far. I enjoyed hitting him. I enjoyed it even more when he tried to take me a second time.'

'You always were a fighter,' she snapped.

'And I still am. Just remember that.'

'I can hardly forget when you go round attacking me all over the place,' she retorted swiftly. 'My arms are black and blue!'

'No, they're not. Don't exaggerate.'

'Well, they soon will be, the way you carry on. Let me *go*!'

'So that you can take another punch at me? You must be joking!'

'I'm not joking—just let me go. I wouldn't soil

my hands on you,' she snapped. 'You're the worst kind of bully—you know you're stronger than me——'

'True,' he murmured. 'I'm glad you realise that, anyway.'

'You keep interrupting me,' she said. 'Oh!—you—you——!'

'Only because you talk so stupid,' he answered. 'One minute you're sophisticated, the next you're like a confused teenager. Grow up, Catriona.'

'I am grown up,' she snapped. 'I'm twenty-five.'

'Then act your age—you're good at acting, remember?'

She relaxed, fractionally. What was the use of arguing? 'And how would you know *that*?' she taunted. 'Don't tell me you've watched me on television?'

'Frequently,' he said drily.

'I'm honoured,' she breathed.

'Are you? You might not be if you knew what I've noticed.'

'And what does that mean?'

'A certain deterioration in performance in your last play.'

'That's a lousy thing to say!'

'It happens to be true. I dare say your many fans wouldn't have noticed a thing, but I did. Actors—actresses—are the people who give my words the flesh and blood, the life. I notice. If you carry on as you are now, in five years you'll be forgotten.'

'I don't have to stand and listen to your spiteful——'

'You don't have to, but you will, because like it or not, deep within yourself you know I speak the truth. Don't you realise what's happening to you?' He had released her arms, she was free, but she wasn't, because his words had the force in them to prevent her moving. 'Don't you *know*?'

'No,' she wanted to deny, to make them not have happened, but there was something about his words. 'No——' She shook her head.

'And he's responsible—Simon Meredith.'

'You hate him!' she burst out.

'I don't *hate* anybody. I *despise* him and the people like him who seek to corrupt.'

'Now I know you're mad!' she gasped. But Lachlan took her and led her to the mirror in the corner of the kitchen.

'Look at yourself,' he said, and, resistance in every inch of her, she did. She saw herself as she always did. 'Soon your looks will be gone. Already you're tired and run down. You flare up easily. You threw a tantrum in your last play——'

'They'd messed the schedules—anyway, how do you know *that*?' she gasped.

'I have—contacts.'

'Spies, you mean! And why spy on *me*? Why me?'

'You'll find out, soon enough.'

'I won't find out a damned thing if you don't tell me!' She turned from the mirror to face him.

'I want to know why this vendetta against me? And if I'm so lousy, why bring *me* here? I've no doubt dozens of aspiring actresses would have jumped at the chance to come with you. Some women would do anything—and I mean *anything* —to get a part in one of your plays. God knows why, there's no accounting for taste.' She could fight back, after all, and she was going to.

'Very probably.' He smiled. She didn't like it when he smiled like that. 'But they wouldn't have done at all. You're the one I wanted.'

'Then why don't you stop criticising me?'

'Is he your lover yet?'

'That's none of your business!' she snapped.

'I suppose not.'

'Would it matter, either way?' She should finish this discussion immediately. She should refuse to listen to, or answer him. But she couldn't.

'No, it wouldn't. I'd like to know.'

'You're not going to. You can *assume* what you like——' She tossed her hair back. 'Want to try *your* luck? No chance, I'm fussy.'

'So they say,' he nodded.

'Who's "they"?'

'Those who're in the business. Remember Damien Ellis?'

Catriona did. He was a handsome actor with whom she had been in a play a year or so ago. He had his reputation as a Casanova to maintain, and had pursued Catriona relentlessly for several months. She had been out with him a few times, but that was all they had been, evenings out. 'Him?' she laughed scornfully. 'Do you know him?' It was like a net closing round her. As though he knew everyone *she* knew.

'I met him once. He was talking about you to someone, and I—listened.'

'And oh, boy, you're good at *that*, aren't you?' she flashed.

'Don't you want to know what he said?' asked Lachlan.

'Not particularly. Actor's gossip is boring.'

'This wasn't.'

'I still don't want to know.' She did.

'I'll tell you anyway. He said you were like the Sleeping Beauty waiting for the Prince to come along. He implied you were clearly not normal——'

'Who is?'

'Allowing for his natural frustration at not being able to bed you, he had a valid point. You are waiting for someone. I wonder who?'

'It's sure as dammit not *you*, anyway,' she breathed.

He reached out and stroked her cheek, fingers lingering on the soft, sweet flesh. Catriona didn't flinch. Although she wanted to scream, she didn't move at all. She wouldn't give him that satisfaction. 'Isn't it?' he said softly. 'It would have been—years ago.'

'*No!*' She couldn't bear that. That was the unforgivable. He had said what should never have been said. Never— She pushed his hand away as though it burned her, and stared at him wide-eyed, face white with shock. 'No!' She shook her head, to make the words go away, and her hair tumbled about her face. She put her hands up to shut out the sight of him and he pulled them away.

He said harshly: 'Oh, yes, Catriona. Don't you know why I left Crannich? It was because of *you*.' She was trembling, helpless and trembling and vulnerable. She felt as if she couldn't breathe—she wanted to run away. Dear God, he too remembered. She had been wrong about that.

'No, it's—it's past now. I don't want to remember.'

'You've never forgotten, have you? Be truthful.'

She shook her head. 'Please—leave me alone,' she pleaded.

Lachlan took his hands from her, then took a deep breath and turned away. It was as though some emotion, too deep to be put into words, filled him. He walked out of the kitchen, out of the back door, and closed it behind him.

Catriona was left on her own. She remained standing where she was. For ten years Lachlan Erskine had been in her mind, and she had never been able to forget him. On the conscious surface, yes. Her life had been busy and successful and, more recently, complicated, and there had been days, even weeks, when she hadn't given him a thought in her waking moments. But he returned to her in dreams. Dreams that were forgotten on waking, and only remembered when and if something triggered off the memory. Perhaps these days here alone with him would exorcise those memories, for how could she ever love a man who would make two harmless old people homeless if she had refused him? That was surely crueller than anything else he could do—even crueller than what he had done ten years ago.

She turned sharply, refusing to allow herself to think of that, and her hand caught the back of a chair and she felt sudden pain and looked to see blood welling from a cut on her index finger. A small nail jutted out from a bad join, and she had sliced her finger open on it. She ran to the hand pump at the sink and depressed it several times until water gushed out. Then she fumbled for her handkerchief in her bag and wrapped it tightly round the finger, clumsily because it was her right hand she had cut. It hurt, but not as much as she did, and in fact it helped to lessen the other, older pain.

The door swung open and Lachlan came in with an armful of logs for the fire, and saw her. He made a small, exasperated sound. 'What have you done?'

'Cut myself. That chair's got a nail sticking out,' she answered.

'Let me see.'

'It's all right—I washed it.'

'Let me *see*.'

Catriona held her hand out. 'I told you it was all right,' she began, and looked in horror at the rapidly reddening handkerchief he was peeling off.

'You'd better sit down,' he said. 'I've got some bandages somewhere,' and he went out. Catriona sat down at the table and pressed the sodden hanky to her finger. Don't let me faint, she prayed. Not again——

He was back with a small plastic holdall which he was unwrapping as he came in. Within one minute she had a neatly covered bandaged finger securely fastened with tape.

'Thank you,' she muttered.

'I'll get the fish cooked,' he said. 'But first——' and he picked up the poker and flattened the offending nail into the chair back. 'That's done. Are you always so accident-prone?'

'No,' she answered.

'That's good. I can cope with minor accidents, but I'm not a doctor.'

'You've got a simple solution to that,' she answered.

'Not yet. We're not leaving yet. We've only just begun.'

'Begun what? The play—or bringing back the—past?'

'Both.'

'I wouldn't have come if I'd known. You have no right——'

'I have every right to do as I choose,' he said.

'No, damn it, you haven't,' she said, in a voice that shook. She clenched her left hand on the table. 'I was fifteen—*fifteen*!'

'And you wanted me to make love to you——'

'No!' Tears sprang to her eyes. 'I—I——' she swallowed. 'If you hadn't followed me, it——'

'I followed you because that man you'd been leading up the garden path had hit you.' He stood looking down at her.

'He was only a student, only twenty—I'd upset him when I'd run out of the village dance the night before.'

'Yes, I know fine well you had. After flirting with him, flaunting yourself all evening, you'd realised you'd gone too far and run off——' he gave a contemptuous smile. 'It's little wonder he was hopping mad when he caught up with you on the beach the day after. Serves you damned well right. You deserved to get your face slapped.'

'Then why did you give him a good hiding?' she sparked back.

'I thought he was going to hit you again.'

'He wasn't. You came rushing up like a——'

'I knocked him flying. I don't regret it. I regret following you though, to see if you were all right.'

'Is that why you kissed me?' she said, white-faced. 'Is that why—you took me in your arms?'

'You'd got me so mad——' He pulled her to her feet. He was angry, nearly shaking with it. She had gone too far, and she knew it, but it was too late to do anything about it. The floodgates had been opened and nothing could close them again. She whimpered, feeling the trembling anger, the controlled violence of him, and it was so like the last time, so like it, that she waited for what must happen next. 'You—I wanted to beat you. I should have done. Anything would have been better than what——' He stopped, his eyes darkened and full of something she thought was pain. 'Dear God,' he muttered, 'when I held you—and you responded like that——'

'No,' she whispered. 'No!'

'Yes, it's too late now—too late not to say you knew what you were doing all right. You were wanton.'

Catriona wanted to cry out, 'But I loved you, don't you *see*—I loved you!' She couldn't. If Lachlan knew that, her last defence against him would be gone. She forced a bitter laugh out instead. 'I didn't notice you protesting.' Oh God, if only he had known the reason she had been flirting with the student, the visitor to Crannich. She had flirted with him—she couldn't even remember his name now—at the village dance because Lachlan had spent the evening ignoring her. She had done it to make *him* jealous because she had had a crush on him for months, and he had scarcely noticed her.

'I'm a man, remember,' Lachlan went on. 'I was a man then, although younger—and more hot-blooded. I'd have had to be made of stone not to have wanted——'

'Wanted? You didn't want me—you—you—pushed me away——' Her mouth trembled. Even now, after a decade, the memory of the sudden rejection still had the power to hurt so deeply that she could scarcely bear it.

'Don't you know why, for God's sake? You were *fifteen*——' He closed his eyes for a second. 'Do I have to spell it out for you?' His mouth contorted with pain. 'I was twenty-two—old enough to know what I was doing, and the consequences.'

He had wanted her. There in the small shepherd's hut to which she had run weeping after the scene on the beach, and where he had found her and taken her into his arms. He would have made love to her, but he had resisted, and walked out, away from her and out of her life, leaving her shattered, her heart broken, and feeling the pain of rejection so greatly that she had wanted to die. And in a way she had never recovered from that. Even now, hearing at last the truth, she knew it was too late. She felt her legs going weak, felt the strength draining from her body. It was as though she were fifteen again, young, unawakened but yearning for she knew not what, yearning to be loved by the man she had dreamt about since, at the age of fourteen, she had discovered that she loved him.

Lachlan had ruined her life. He didn't know it, but he had. 'Let me go,' she whispered. 'Please let me go,' and the hot tears scalded down her cheeks, and as he released her she turned away and sank into the chair and huddled away from him, hurting, aching all over.

'Oh God, Catriona!' He knelt beside the chair and she shrank away from him.

'No! Please—keep away from me. Please—I beg

of you,' she whispered. She was like a wounded animal, she wanted to go away and lick her wounds in private. Because of him, and what he had done, she had never allowed herself to want any man. For what if she did, and then he didn't want her, and walked away? He had brought her here, a woman of twenty-five, mature, outwardly attractive and successful, and he was cruel, first by the means of persuasion he had used, and secondly by what he had just said, expressing that which she had buried deep. She knew why, quite suddenly. It was so that he would write a play better than any he had done before. By tearing her emotions raw he would succeed, he would watch her, use her—he would use her, as he must use everybody.

He had moved away after her plea, and was standing not far from her, and she knew he was watching her, even without looking up. She was aware of his eyes on her. He was probably making mental notes now, finding a satisfaction in her unhappiness. There was nothing she could do about it, for she lacked any strength at that moment. She was at her lowest ebb, and it was as she realised it that she knew she must fight back, and regain her self-respect. When you have reached the bottom, there is only one way to go.

She looked up slowly. 'I hope you're satisfied,' she said quietly. She stood up, carefully, lest she fall. 'I'm all right now. Sorry to disappoint you, but there'll be no more hysterics.' She even managed a smile. Lachlan didn't look satisfied, he looked like a man who had been struck hard. His face was white; with temper, or shock? Catriona didn't really care any more. The ghosts of the past were gone. She would never dream about him again. When she left here, she was going to begin to live, and she would never think of him again.

She took a deep breath. 'Are we having lunch?' she asked.

'I'll do it. You can't with your hand.'

'Very well. I want to go for a walk—alone.' She took her coat from the hook by the door, opened it and went outside. The mist was thicker than ever, and visibility was limited, but she could see well enough. She went out of the gate, along to the shore. Only the first few yards of the water were visible, the rest was a grey sweeping waste. The mist was wet, it clung to her hair and her clothes as she made her way along the shingles, with only the crunching sound of her footsteps for company.

Gradually she began to think of the actress alone there, deciding whether to live or to die, and she knew now how the character would feel, and perhaps that was why Lachlan had done it. He would get his play. It would be her gift to him for releasing her from the past.

There would be someone in hiding, watching her pass, following her, keeping always out of sight— not difficult in this, and he too would be a haunted creature on the run, wondering if she was sent as a trap for him, the only difference being that he wanted to live, to escape only from his past, not himself. The thoughts were so real, the theme so gripping that she found to her horror that she was listening for other sounds—other footsteps. She stopped. Silence. Complete and utter stillness. What would his name be? He had to have a name for him. Or would he just be The Man? She began to see it as it would be on television. The hotel was an ideal setting for the interiors. The empty rooms, dusty and abandoned after years. No electricity, only lamps, that had to be carried from room to room—and then, one day, the meeting, when perhaps he realised that she was truly alone, and he would step forward one night, as she sat in the kitchen by the fire, and tell her not to be afraid. How would she react? Utter terror at first, followed by acceptance.

She could see it as real as if she were watching it on a screen. It would be a powerful play.

It was time to turn back. If she stayed out any longer Lachlan might come looking for her, and she didn't want that. She began to retrace her steps, and she thought how strange it would be if someone else *was* on the island, listening. She walked more quickly. She wasn't frightened, and it was absurd, but she wanted to be back in that warm kitchen where she would be safe.

Surely she hadn't walked this far? Where was it? She couldn't see anything at all on either side, the mist was thicker, so thick—— She began to run as if pursued, her heartbeats a wild crescendo, her feet a blur on the rough shingle, not looking back, not daring to look behind——

It was there. She ran in the front door, slammed it, shut, ran across the hall to the kitchen—and it was empty. Catriona stood there leaning against the door, panting, getting her breath back, and it was as though she were really alone—all alone—alone...

She heard footsteps behind her from the passage and turned from the door and faced it, fearful of what she would see.

Lachlan walked in, stopped when he saw her. 'What is it?' he demanded. She nearly fell into his arms, and he held her, and repeated his question.

'I thought——' She could hardly speak, then it all came pouring out, and she was aware, belatedly, that she had run into his arms in a sheer relief from terror, and that he held her comfortingly, and when she had finished telling him she took a deep shuddering breath.

'I'm sorry,' he said. 'I didn't mean the play to have this effect on you,' but he still held her.

'It was stupid, I know.' She could still feel her heart pounding. Perhaps he could too. 'But when I came in and you weren't here—and for a moment it was as though I *was* alone——'

'I'd only gone to see to the heaters. I heard you run in as though someone was after you, so I came straight back,' he said. 'You're trembling like a leaf.' He eased her coat off as he said it, but retained his hold on her.

Catriona was too. 'I'll be all right in a moment,'

she murmured. She looked up at him. 'Really, I'm——' There was an instant, as their eyes met, and she stopped, and it was as though time itself stopped. And neither moved nor spoke, not for this timeless moment, until, as if obeying some inevitable law, they both moved, their lips meeting softly, gently, then more firmly, clinging, holding each to the other, lost, helpless, blending and melting with the surging fire that filled them both.

Catriona was trembling, not now with fear, but with the sweet wild longing that had no name, and she was held in his arms, and hers were round his neck, and she felt herself being lifted, carried back through a door and into her bedroom. They sank down on to the bed, slowly, gently, lying down together, arms and legs entwined, his mouth on hers, his body hard and muscular, and there was no one here, and she wasn't fifteen any more, and Lachlan was going to make love to her, and this time he wouldn't run away. He unbuttoned the tunic she wore, slowly, so slowly, and eased it off, and looked at her, his eyes travelling from her face to her breasts, back again, then a slow, gentle smile, and the light blotted out as his face came down on hers, and all was sweet sensation and longing. Gently easing themselves under the covers, and he with his sweater off, hard muscular chest against hers, the hairs tickling her, he rubbing himself against her, sensuous, hard bodied, no resistance left on either side. She moaned softly as he unfastened her bra, and ran her tongue across her lips. The fire was there now, under the covers, all was burning, burning, and she moved herself slightly away and held his head, guiding it to her breasts, her breathing shallow, panting. She closed her eyes in ecstasy as his lips moved on one, and held his head, feeling the shaggy hair under her guiding hands. His hands were elsewhere, teasing, caressing, undressing skilfully, seeking, finding, hard hands that were gentle now ...

'Mmm,' she murmured, and he laughed softly and ran a trail with his tongue up to her neck, kissed it, then her chin, then her mouth. His hands bruised her flesh, seeking hands, going where they needed to, stroking, smoothing, curving round and down and up ...

Then she saw the ceiling, saw the familiar pattern of the heater, and knew the sweet smell of the paraffin, and knew that he had lit it because this was what he had planned. The sudden shock made her stiffen, go cold inside. She pushed him away with a wordless exclamation, looked at him lying there, his face dark with desire, his arms ready to take her again, to possess her as he intended to possess her with his body. Planned, like everything else had been. 'No!' she exclaimed. 'Oh no—not this as well——!' She almost fell out of the bed, grabbing for her tunic, zipping up her pants, and Lachlan heaved himself up and looked at her as if stunned.

'You'd got it planned!' she spat. 'Just like everything else. Oh God, is that what happens in the play as well? Are we to live it all?' She was sobbing as she buttoned up the tunic, fingers clumsy with the bandage, then she put her shoes on and ran out, along the passage to the front, opened the door and ran along away from the hotel. She heard Lachlan's voice calling her, then that was lost. On and on she ran, not knowing or caring where she was going, her only thought, escape.

A rock loomed up and she swerved to avoid it and went flying, skidding on the damp shale, tumbling down towards the water, rolling, falling, until half stunned, she came to a halt and felt the water lapping at her arms as she lay there unable for the moment to move. It was icy cold. She had to get away from there before she froze.

She heard his voice calling her, shouting to her—she tasted sea water. The world was a strange dark place.

'Lachlan,' she muttered, gathering her strength for the last feeble effort. The tide was coming in. It was lapping at her shoulders, touching her hair——

She was being lifted, very carefully, very gently—not like his words. 'You mad fool!' he shouted, shaking with anger. 'What the hell do you think you're doing? Trying to kill yourself?' He was carrying her back, walking quickly. She was drenched and frozen, hating both him and herself. Herself most of all.

He put her on the bed. 'Don't move,' he said. 'I'm going to get a towel and dry you, and if you move I'll give you such a hiding, so help me, you'll wish you'd drowned!' He slammed out and returned a moment later, with a towel and a large warm sweater, which he flung on the bed. Then he was easing off her tunic, rubbing her with the towel, face, hair, shoulders, body. He put the sweater on her, eased off her pants, pulled the bedclothes over her and went out again.

When he returned he was carrying two hot water bottles and a beaker with whisky in. 'Drink that,' he said.

'I don't——'

'*Drink it!*' he ordered. Catriona swallowed it in one and lay back and he tucked the bottles in beside her and sat on the bed. 'You bloody fool,' he said angrily. 'You absolute stupid idiot—you want a good hiding!'

'You'd planned it,' she said wildly. 'You'd planned it all—I can see that now. You m-must think I'm stupid!'

'What the hell are you talking about?' he said.

'The heater in here—you put it on—it was what you——'

'Don't be so damn stupid! Did I "plan" to have you fling yourself in my arms after your walk? I put the heater on for you, for tonight, because it had gone so cold. Is that why——' he stopped. 'Is *that* what you thought?'

'Yes.'

Lachlan stood up. 'I see. Thanks.' He walked out and closed the door.

CHAPTER SIX

CATRIONA lay there until hunger compelled her to move. She left the sweater on that Lachlan had brought. It was one of his, and far too big, but she didn't care. She found another pair of pants, put them on and went out to the kitchen.

There was a note on the table. 'Your dinner's in the oven, L.'. That was all. His coat had gone from the door, and she could see why. The mist now totally obscured vision from the windows, and the kitchen was cold, the fire having died down. She put on more logs and brought a plate of fish, carrots and potatoes from the oven. It was hot and she nearly dropped it. She put it on the table and began to eat. It was nearly three. She had no idea how long Lachlan had been gone, or when he would be back, or even where he had gone to.

He had been angry when he had walked out on her—more angry than she had ever seen him before, his voice bitter and caustic. She read the note again. His writing was blunt and decisive, almost slashed on to the page. She crumpled it up and threw it in the fire, then finished her dinner.

Now what? She looked around. There was no radio, no books to read—nothing. She hadn't even brought her play script with her. She didn't want to sit and do nothing, or she would go mad. What would the other Catriona have done, the one in the play? Taken long walks, probably, but she wasn't going to chance that, not in this, and she still ached from the fall. Her side was bruised and sore, and she had grazed her hands in trying to save herself. She took a deep breath. The tape recorder was on a cupboard top, and there were two batteries and two tapes beside it.

She switched it on and ran back the tape in it to the beginning and set it to play. It was surprising to hear her voice describing her reactions to the hotel, and the sense of fear she had had in one room. Because it all came pouring out of her, and she hadn't heard it replayed, it was like hearing someone else talking. The tape recorder, being a small one, distorted her voice slightly so that it was like hearing a stranger, and despite herself, she was fascinated by it. When it came to the point where Lachlan had switched it off, she stopped it. The hearing of it again had given her an idea. Why not go on? Imagine the other Catriona's reaction when she met the fugitive for the first time. First, though, she had to picture him. She had no idea what Lachlan planned, but she could have her own image of a man for now, and see what happened. This exercise was much easier than going over what had so nearly happened a short time ago.

She rested her chin on her palm. He had been here how long? A week or two? He would have a beard, and his clothes would be rough. She tried to picture him, and saw Lachlan's face—all right, let it be like him. A beard would suit him. He would have to have a name. Her mind went blank, and she looked round the room as if for inspiration. Good grief, there were dozens—there must be! She made herself think of Russian playwrights, composers—Borodin—*Prince Igor*. Igor! That would do—for now anyway.

Right, she thought, I'm sitting alone, it's evening, I've eaten—and something's bothering me. What? Inspiration struck. Of course, she thought, I've eaten, and before, when I went to prepare a meal from my meagre store, *something was missing*. But what? What would an actress who didn't really care whether she lived or died bring to eat? Fruit probably, cheese, eggs, small tins of meat and vegetables. Cheese. That's it. I'd brought two supermarket packs of cheese, and one had gone.

She felt a tingle of excitement. The food they had brought with them—and what Lachlan had also brought on his previous visit—were in a cupboard. Catriona went slowly over to it, and it seemed that the cameras were turning and there was an invisible director telling her to act. She opened the cupboard, searched, frowned, looked again, took out the cellophane-wrapped portion of Cheshire cheese, and looked at it. 'There were two here,' she said, and turned, eyes scanning every kitchen surface. 'I *know* there were.' Her face registered the puzzlement she was now genuinely feeling, and she turned back to the cupboard and brought out everything, her movements quick and jerky, searching desperately for the missing food. 'Oh God,' she whispered. 'It can't have——'

This would be the ideal moment for the man to enter. Listening to her, outside the door, knowing that his theft had been discovered. He would be hungry. What would he have lived on? Fish, obviously the main item. But what else? Then she remembered. It seemed important to write everything down while it was fresh in her mind. Lachlan's notebook was on the cupboard by the tapes. She opened it at the back, where the page was blank, found the pen, and began to write. She looked with satisfaction at the short list when she had finished. If he objected it was just too bad. She'd buy him a new notebook. He might even add to her list.

Back to the play. There she was, alone, just having discovered some food missing, and knowing it was impossible—but it had happened, and the door opened slowly, and a man stood there. She looked at the closed door and pictured an older Lachlan standing there, rough, bearded. Just watching her. She stepped back, eyes seeking for a weapon, darted to the poker, and held it up. 'Who are you?' she demanded, eyes wide with fear.

Lachlan walked in behind her, from the other door, and she turned, screamed, and dropped the poker. 'Oh!' she gasped.

His face was cold and hard. 'I take it you were waiting for me with that,' he said. 'Sorry I came in the wrong way.'

The small bubble of excitement burst. Somehow, without being sure why, she had wanted to please him, and it had seemed such a good idea. She picked up the poker and replaced it. He saw the tape recorder, the open exercise book, and Catriona explained: 'I—didn't know how long you'd be. I was just going over a scene in my mind, ready for—for—to help.'

'Were you?' He picked up his exercise book. 'What's this? "Nettles, dandelions, seaweed?"'

'Well, I was imagining her—the actress—on her own here, and then discovering that some food had been stolen, obviously by Igor——'

'Igor?' He raised an eyebrow. 'Why Igor?'

'I had to give him a name so that I could think about him, and picture him, you see.'

He wasn't making it easy for her. He stood there listening, polite but blank. 'Really? And how do you picture him?'

'Well, if he's been here a while, he'll have a beard—I mean, he'll hardly have swum all this way carrying his luggage—and I sort of pictured him like you only older. It seemed—er—easier.' She felt foolish.

'Go on,' he said, and began to shrug his coat off. At least he didn't seem very angry—nor laughing at her, which she supposed was something.

'Well, then I just began to imagine a scene where he comes in—and how she'd react. I'd just grabbed the poker. He was standing at that other door, and you walked in.'

'I see. And where do nettles fit into this?'

'Oh well, I thought about what *he'd* be living on. Obviously fish—then I wondered what other kinds of food there'd be on an island like this, and that's what I came up with. I know it won't go into the play, but it——' she shrugged, 'seems to help.'

'Okay.' Lachlan sat down. 'Let's act out your little scene. That is what you wanted, isn't it?'

'It's not my play. You're doing it.'

'Then why do you make up scenes?'

'There was nothing else to do,' she retorted. Damn him! It was supposed to be what he'd brought her here for. '*You'd* gone out.'

'I'd gone out to cool down. It was either that or strangle you.' He regarded her very levelly, and a muscle moved in his cheek.

'Because your seduction scene went wrong? Tough! I don't suppose you're used to getting "no" for an answer,' she snapped. Two spots of colour burned in her cheeks.

'Not at that stage, no. And you won't get anywhere by throwing a temper,' he said.

'I am not throwing a temper,' she said. 'I don't want to talk about it.'

'You brought the subject up.' Tension filled the room, sudden vibrant tension like an electric current. Catriona caught her breath, strongly aware of it, tingling at her nerve ends. His anger was a potent force, as strong as he, and she had no weapons to fight it. She stood there, the temper draining away from her in the face of his, and she didn't know how to cope, because she had never known anybody else like him; he was far stronger than anyone she had ever known, far stronger than the young man who had walked away from her that day, long ago, and never forgotten.

She hated him and she loved him all at the same time, and the feelings were so strong, so nearly overwhelming, that she felt weak with them. She should have made love with him. It would have been so different now. She wanted to, that was the terrible thing. She wanted him to take her, to possess her——

She sat down at the table. 'I'm sorry,' she said quietly.

'For what? Yourself—or me—or the accusation?'

'For making you angry.'

'What makes you think that?' His voice was heavy with sarcasm. It bit deep into her already raw emotions, and she winced. 'Me—angry? Why should I be?' He laughed. 'You're no different now from what you were ten years ago. There's a name for women like you, but I won't use it——'

'Don't,' she said. 'Please!' Tears sprang to her eyes.

'Don't bother with the tears. I've seen you do that, very nicely, in one of your plays. You can turn the taps on at will, can't you? It's quite an advantage for an actress—saves the glycerine drops.'

'I'm not——' she choked them back. 'You're cruel!'

'I haven't even begun to be cruel,' he cut in.

'I was trying—to please you, to help you—I thought that's what we came here for,' she answered, fighting to retain her control.

'It was—partly—but I don't think it's going to work,' he said, each word clear and emphatic. 'You get me madder than anyone has a right to.'

'I don't do it on purpose. You don't do so badly at that yourself, either,' she retorted. 'You're aggressive—you accuse me of having a temper, but by golly, you want to hear yourself some time!' She jumped to her feet. 'You make me sick! Do you hear—*sick!*' She turned away and went to the sink. 'And I'm damned if I'm going to walk out every time you do that. I get you mad! Good! If I got you mad enough perhaps we could go home,' and she banged the kettle on to the gas. She was shaking with anger. Who the *hell* did he think he was, laying down the law, telling her what to do? She turned to him as he got to his feet. He looked as though he was capable of striking her. He looked capable of anything.

Something, a wave of despair, came over her. 'Oh God,' she groaned. 'What are we trying to do to each other? Destroy ourselves? I can't take much more, Lachlan.' The words came pouring out. 'When my grandmother's letter came I was in a state of exhaustion. I needed that letter in a way. It decided me what to do. Otherwise I would have had to get away. I was exhausted, sleeping badly, having nightmares—and I—came up, expecting peace and quiet—and instead—this.' She looked at him, her face drawn and pale, and saw the expression on his as well, and wanted to cry out. 'I—I can't——' she paused. 'I know you think I'm acting all the time, but I'm not. I don't know any other way to say it, I'm so tired, so very tired—and I can't go on like this, as I am doing, tearing myself apart——' She brushed her hair from her face with a trembling hand. 'I'm sorry—I'm sorry for everything, but please—stop being so angry with me——' her voice broke. 'Please,' she whispered.

She saw the look in his eyes, the deep pain that was there. Then he moved slowly towards her, reached out and took her in his arms. There was no anger in him, only, it seemed, a despair to match her own. Wordlessly he held her for moments, or it might have been minutes, and no words were needed any more, they had all been said. She felt his heart beating steady and strong, and in his arms, and the strength of them, was the solace she sought. For the first time ever, the tension had disappeared.

'It's all right,' he said, at last. 'It's all right, Catriona.'

She raised her face to his, her cheeks wet with tears, and she saw him looking down at her, and he wasn't smiling. He looked as though he would never smile again. He looked—tormented. She made a small sound and touched his face, sadly, softly. 'No,' she whispered. 'Don't—don't look like that.'

'Don't you know why?' he said, his voice scarcely more than a murmur. 'Dear God, don't you know why?'

A tremor filled her. 'No,' she said, 'I don't.'

Lachlan stroked her hair with a gentle, careful hand, then sighed. It was a sigh that held all the burdens of the world in it. 'It's no use,' he said. 'I thought—if we came here—if we had time together, alone, we could see——' His mouth twisted. 'And all we do is fight.'

'Could see what?' she asked.

'See things straight for once, both of us, after so long a time.'

'I don't know what you're saying.' She looked at him, bewildered. There was no question of either of them moving away from each other. It was as though a truce had been called, a certain peace in the middle of strife. She didn't question it. Her heartfelt plea had worked, at least she had that.

'Dear girl, you've been in my mind, so much a part of me, for years. When I saw what was happening to you in London I had to do something. I could no longer wait for the right moment.'

Catriona shook her head. '*You* thought of *me*?'

'Does it sound strange? It's not to me.' He pulled her towards him, close, closer, tightly. 'God, I've loved you, wanted you——'

'Lachlan, don't be more cruel——' She tried to pull herself away, sickened by his words. Infinitely cruel, but more cruel than he imagined because of her own feelings.

'Cruel?' he echoed. 'Do you think I'm *joking*?'

'It's not funny,' she began, trembling.

'It's not meant to be,' he grated, and, as if drawn irresistibly, he crushed her to him and began to kiss her—at first despairingly, then gradually the tenor changed, and his lips were hungry on hers, searching, seeking, and she responded hungrily, matching his growing excitement with her own as she realised, at last, what she should have known from that first moment of seeing him in the woods.

Swept along on a warm tide of sweet longing, no more barriers between them, the aching emptiness, the brittle antagonism, all were removed in the endless moments that passed and they clung together, knowing now that this was the only reality. This was the only reality there had ever been for either of them.

Lachlan had been in her mind for so many years, as much a part of her as her own body, her own being—and now, at last she knew the truth of what had happened all that time ago between them, she knew the sweet inevitability of it all—and it was a dream coming to fruition. Something had begun, ten years previously, something that had lain dormant, sleeping, not yet ready to awaken, but always there—and it hadn't been one-sided after all. It had not just been something that was a part of her, but a part of him also. She knew that as well now, and there was a richness and beauty in the knowledge, and her heart was full, and she knew the flowering of a love that was now ripe, and ready.

'Lachlan,' she murmured, minutes, aeons later, when he released her and began to breathe again, 'are we both dreaming?'

'I don't think so,' he answered. He stood there,

looking at her, eyes soft with love, and he smiled in a way she had never seen him smile before. 'If we are, let's hope we don't wake up. Oh, darling Catriona, what absolute fools we've been all this time!'

She put her hands up to his face, to feel the hard smooth skin beneath her fingers, and he turned and bit her thumb gently, nuzzling it, and she laughed. 'I've got a confession,' he told her.

'What?' For a moment her heart stopped, but she saw his face, saw the twitch of his mouth, and it was all right.

'The method I used—the "blackmail". It wasn't.'

'You mean——'

'I mean I had no intention of putting your grandparents out.'

'Oh!' She shook her head. 'I believed you!'

'I meant you to.' Lachlan cupped her chin. 'You're so beautiful to me, so very beautiful, Catriona. Everything about you——' He kissed her nose gently. 'Especially your nose.'

'You're an idiot,' she giggled.

'Mmm, I know. So are you. You're not fighting me any more. I wonder why?'

'I can't beat you. I knew that a while ago.'

'Good. Is that the only reason?'

'No—o,' she hesitated.

'So?'

'I love you, Lachlan, I've always loved you,' she whispered.

'That's what I wanted to hear,' he said, and sighed. 'That's all I wanted to hear. Let's go back home to Crannich.'

'Now? What about the play?'

'Damn that. I can write that anywhere—if you're with me.'

'We can't leave in this.' They both turned, and walking arms entwined, went to the door. Lachlan opened it, and the mist billowed in, icy cold, clinging. He slammed the door.

'No.' He looked down at her. 'Hmmm, I can't think of anything else to do, can you?'

Catriona felt a warm tide of colour suffuse her face and shook her head. 'Do some work on the play?' she suggested, trying not to laugh. He lifted her up and swung her round and she cried, 'Oh! Ouch!'

'What is it?' He put her down instantly.

'I ache all over with falling—outside.'

'My little precious one! I can't have you hurt! You'd better let me see.' His mouth was twitching.

'I think not,' she said, but faintly.

He bent his head, as if he hadn't heard her. 'What did you say?'

'I said—um—better not.'

Lachlan stroked her sides gently. 'I'm a very good nurse,' he said. Her heart was thudding. His hands continued their gentle massage, thoughtfully, consideringly, and he frowned slightly as if worried. 'Mmm, could be serious,' he said, 'if not attended to.'

'I'll get over it, I'm sure.' Her voice was growing quieter. It really was quite difficult to answer him while his hands were at their work. She cleared her throat. 'It's better already.'

'I'm so glad,' he whispered, as he bent his head. 'Truly, very glad about that,' but he didn't stop, and Catriona said, even more faintly, after a few more moments:

'I didn't hurt myself *there*!'

'No? Oh, sorry—never mind, though——'

'Lachlan,' she managed to say, 'we shouldn't be——'

'I want to make love to you, Catriona. I've ached to make love to you ever since that day.'

'But I'm—frightened,' she whispered.

'Dear God, of me?'

'No.'

He moved back slightly, looked at her. 'I love you so much, Catriona—but we'll wait. We've all the time in the world now, don't you see? Will you marry me, my love?'

She trembled. 'Do you need to ask?'

'Yes, I want to hear you say it.'

'Oh yes—yes!'

'All the more reason why we should get back,' he said tenderly. 'You've already had a disastrous effect on my self-control. I won't be responsible for anything if we stay here much longer.'

'Did you really feel like strangling me?'

He laughed softly. 'Either that or giving you a good hiding—I went for a long walk and kicked a few stones. It didn't do a lot for my feet, but it cooled me down.' He picked her up in his arms, and as she clutched him in alarm, grinned. 'You're safe,' he told her. 'Very safe, I just want to *hold* you— Oh God, it's wonderful to have you in my arms!' He lifted her high and she squealed in alarm.

'You don't know your own strength,' she gasped.

'Oh yes, I do.' He put her down and slapped her bottom. 'I'm hungry. Get my meal ready, woman.'

'Good grief, it's only five!'

'Never mind. We'll eat, then talk over the play— because I need something to take my mind off you, and that's the only thing guaranteed to do it, and then, later tonight, we'll talk about our future. Together.'

'Yes, oh, master.' She curtsied. 'Go and sit down.'

She went to the food cupboard, her heart singing. All the agonies, the traumas, all were gone, smoothed away as if they had never been. She tingled with happiness, and hummed softly as she prepared a simple meal of ham and salad. The eggs were boiling and she was washing lettuce when she sensed Lachlan's movement behind her, and the next moment his arms came round her waist, his head was on her shoulder and he was nibbling at her ear.

'How do you expect me to prepare your meal like this?' she murmured breathlessly, leaning back to touch his hard body.

'You'll have to improvise,' he whispered. 'That sweater suits you. A little baggy, but elegant.'

She chuckled. 'Want it back?'

'Not yet.' He spoke as if giving the matter serious

consideration. 'Not just yet.'

'That's good. It's too cold to take it off.'

His hands slid up beneath it. 'You don't *feel* cold,' he said thoughtfully.

'Not—mmm—cold at all.'

Catriona went very still, forgetting the lettuce, forgetting everything ... Very casually Lachlan turned the gas off, and he had to lean over to do it, and she said: 'They're for our salad——'

'I'm not hungry.'

'But you said——'

Slowly she turned round, not sure whether she was moving of her own volition or being gently manipulated, and it didn't matter anyway. She had her back to the sink, and she couldn't escape even if she wanted to, but she didn't want to.

'Lachlan,' she said, some time later, 'isn't it going a bit cold in here?'

He looked round at the fire. 'I'm quite warm.'

'The fire's nearly out,' she murmured.

'So it is.' He bent to kiss the rapid pulse beating in her neck. 'I'll keep you warm.'

'My legs are tired.'

He looked concerned, but he was fighting back a smile. 'Hmm,' he mused, and ran his finger down her cheek. 'Do you want to lie down somewhere?'

'I wouldn't mind,' she whispered. 'Just that, you understand?'

'Of course I understand,' he said soothingly. 'You had a nasty fall and you need a rest. I'll keep you company.'

They walked through into her bedroom, and she kicked off her shoes and lay down, he followed her, and lay beside her. 'That better?' he enquired solicitously.

'Much.' She stretched luxuriously. 'Look out of the window. It's pitch black outside.'

'It's not so light in here,' he answered. 'Want the lamp in?'

'No—o. Let's just talk.'

'Talk? Is that all you want to do?'

'I want you to hold me,' she whispered, 'and keep me warm and safe.' Lachlan pulled the covers over them, and for several minutes they lay in companionable silence, and she wondered how to tell him what she must tell him. He kissed her gently, and she responded. She didn't want him to be angry. She never wanted him angry again, and here, he might not be. Not if she told him in the right way. But how to start? When his arm crept slowly round her, caressing and warm, she said: 'Lachlan——'

'Mmm?'

'There's something I must tell you.'

'Fire away. You have a captive audience, my darling.'

She took a desperate breath. 'I've never—made love—I——' She paused. 'I—I'm frightened.'

'Of what? Men? Me?'

'I don't know,' she whispered, and eased herself round to face him. 'That's the awful thing. I don't know, I've—been blaming you, because of—you know, that day, but now I'm honestly not sure. I don't think it's that.'

'You're frightened of being possessed, is that it?'

'I don't know,' she said miserably. 'But if we're going to be married——'

'You're scared?' he said gently.

Catriona took a deep breath. 'Yes.'

'I'll be very gentle,' he said. 'Very, very gentle.'

'You're experienced?'

He laughed very softly. 'Oh, my love, I couldn't lie to you. I'm not made of stone, nor am I of a monastic inclination. I've had—affairs—but nothing—no one important.'

She listened. She heard, and it was only what she had expected, and for some reason the way he said the words stayed in her mind—and she was to remember them, much later ... 'Oh, I see,' she murmured. 'Do you think I'm stupid?'

'No, I think you're wonderful. I'll be a—careful teacher, darling, never fear.' He paused. 'Catriona, this conversation is having a disastrous effect on me. Could we change the subject? Like—the weather, for instance?'

She giggled, suddenly happy, and held him tightly. 'It's *foggy*,' she said fiercely.

'Good gracious, is *that* what it is? I thought the windows needed cleaning.'

'You're a fool,' she said.

'A fool in love. Yes, I suppose I am,' he agreed. 'Kiss me.'

'Do you think I ought to?' she asked.

'I'll let you know when you have.'

'It'll be too late then,' she murmured.

'I know. Let's live dangerously,' he whispered, and his lips found hers in a new kind of wonder, a growing, searching wonder that quite suddenly changed, became deeper, more intense. For wordless minutes their lips told each other what was important, and by the time she realised that she shouldn't have come here with him it was too late to matter.

The bedroom was warm with the heater. But it wouldn't have mattered if it had been freezing. There was another kind of heat there, a burning wave that grew more intense until it was a fiery blaze that wouldn't be extinguished. Catriona was helpless with longing, swept along, intense, on a summit now, knowing at last, knowing that this, after all, was what she had been waiting ten long years to experience. There was no fear, only ecstasy, and wonder.

CHAPTER SEVEN

IT was late evening. The fire burnt brightly in the hearth, the room was cosy and warm, and Catriona and Lachlan sat by it on the rug and made their plans. He sat with his arm round her shoulder, and she leaned against him, drawing strength from him, feeling complete, feeling happier than she had ever done in her life. She yawned, and he asked: 'Tired?'

'A little,' she confessed. 'Want a drink before bedtime?'

'I wouldn't mind.'

'Do you ever refuse anything?' she teased.

'Never.' He caught her hand as she stood up. 'Never,' he repeated. 'So you'd better remember that.'

'I will.' She bent to kiss the top of his head. His hair tasted salty, and she rubbed her nose in it. 'Mmm, smells like you've washed your hair in the sea,' she murmured.

He groaned. 'That does things to me. Stop at once!'

She laughed, tapped him, and went to put the kettle on. The mist was vanishing fast, and a fine rain blurred the windows instead. She turned to tell him, and he was watching her, just watching her as if he couldn't take his eyes from her. She smiled and turned away.

'What's the matter? Don't you like me looking?' he asked.

'I love it.' She turned to him again and struck a pose, hand on hip, head tilted back. 'Go on, stare.'

He laughed. 'I'm going to enjoy being married to you,' he said. 'You realise all my plays in future are going to be written for you?'

She dropped the pose, stared at him. 'Good grief! Even the one—the island one?'

He stood up slowly. 'I've a confession to make.'

'Not another one!'

He came over to her. 'It's already written.'

Whatever she had expected, it wasn't that. She looked at him, her mouth slowly opening. 'You mean—all the time I was busy thinking, and you were——' she gestured helplessly towards the tape recorder—'doing that, it didn't matter?'

'No.' He caught hold of her and pulled her to him. 'Angry?'

She shook her head. 'No. Have you brought it?'

'It's locked in my case.'

'Can I read it?'

'Yes. Tonight if you like.' He kissed her. 'I want you to be in it.'

'Lachlan, when we're married—what about my acting? Do you want me to give it up?'

'No, only if you want to. Except——' he paused. 'I want children. I hope you do.'

'Yes, of course.' She could think of nothing she

wanted more.

'Then, of course, things will be different. Until then, though, you'll work as you wish.' He looked down at her. 'Did you really think I'd expect you to give up?'

Catriona shook her head. 'I only want what you want,' she murmured.

'I'm not your old-fashioned man, you know,' he told her. 'Our marriage will be a partnership— except one thing. Whatever you make's your own. *I* support you.'

'I knew there was a touch of male chauvinist piggery somewhere.' She laughed. 'I'll have the best of both worlds, won't I?'

'You'll have the best of everything,' he murmured. 'I'd like to live on Crannich part of the year. I can write well there, away from the bustle.'

'Anything you want,' she agreed.

They looked out of the window as a loud rattle drummed the glass. The rain fell heavily and steadily down. 'We'll be able to leave tomorrow,' Lachlan said. 'This'll clear the mist. Catriona, when we return I want to go down to London for a couple of days, to sort out a few problems—clear the ground, as it were, so that I can return with no worries.'

'Do you want me to come with you?'

'Do you want to?' He smiled down at her.

She should have said yes. She knew that, but only when it was too late. But she didn't know then. 'No, I'll stay with my grandparents. I've only just arrived, after all. You won't be away long? I don't want——' She bit her lip.

'I don't want to leave you,' he said. 'But there are some minor irritations that can't be sorted out by phone. I'll be two days at most. I'll drive to Edinburgh and fly from there.'

Catriona sighed. His life must be a busy one. She accepted that. And it was sensible for him to go if it meant they could make their arrangements after with easy minds. 'You'll phone me?'

'Every hour on the hour,' he said solemnly.

'Idiot!' She hugged him. 'I'll make the drinks. Why don't you go and get the play?'

Lachlan stood back and saluted smartly. 'At once, ma'am.'

She watched him go, bearing one lamp, and smiled to herself. Then she turned back to her task.

It was past midnight when she finished the play he had brought in for her. They had sat in silence in the kitchen, Lachlan lounging back in the battered easy chair, Catriona at the table, the lamp positioned so that the light fell on the pile of typewritten sheets.

She reached the last page, read it, then looked up. Lachlan opened his eyes as if aware of her slight movement. She felt shattered, as if she had been through a never-to-be-forgotten experience, drained and shaken by the power of a play that was without doubt the best thing he had ever written. She felt strangely humbled at the privilege of being the first person to have seen it.

'Well?' he said, gently enquiring.

'Lachlan, it's superb!' She smoothed her hair back. 'I'm exhausted! It's the best thing you've ever done.'

'And you'd like to be the woman?'

She nodded. 'I'd kill you if you let anyone else do it. It's *marvellous*.'

'It was written for you. I saw you in every line I wrote. It's *yours*.'

'The last scene, where they part—it couldn't have happened any other way. I kept thinking, all the way through, that it might have a happy ending, but—it was inevitable——' She shivered. 'It's a powerful play.'

'They'd saved each other,' he said quietly.

'And you know that they'll never forget each other,' she said. 'You *know* that, it's implicit in every line. Whatever she goes on to do, in the future, will be for him, because he saved her.' She sighed. 'I can see it now, on television.'

Lachlan got up and stretched. 'When it's on, we'll be watching it together, remember that.'

The rain had been growing heavier, and there was a sudden flash of lightning that lit the kitchen with eerie blue light. It was followed within seconds by a crash of thunder so violent that it seemed to rumble within the room. Catriona jumped, and he put a hand on her shoulder.

'Scared?' he teased.

'No.' She looked up at him. 'Not with you here.'

'Good.' He bent and kissed her. 'Time for bed.'

They looked at each other. 'Yes,' she said.

He damped the fire down, and she washed their beakers and left them to dry, then she put his play away on the cupboard, with the tape recorder, and picked up her bag. 'I'll go and wash,' she said.

'I'll bring you in a drop of whisky,' he said, 'to help you sleep in the storm.'

'Thank you,' she replied, and went quietly out of the room. She was sitting up in bed when he tapped on the door and came in carrying two beakers. He sat on the bed.

'Cheers,' he said, and raised his beaker.

'Cheers,' she answered. He put out his free hand and held hers.

'All right, love?' he asked.

Catriona nodded. Slowly and carefully Lachlan put down his beaker on the floor, then lifted his hands to cup her face. Steadily he looked at her, and the light from the paraffin lamp was warm, and soft gold, casting the shadows away, chasing them to the far reaches of the room. They were in the golden centre of a pool of light. His eyes searched her face as if imprinting every inch of it in his mind.

'You're truly lovely,' he murmured softly. 'You have a soft inner glow, a warmth in you. I think I must have loved you for as far back as I can remember—and wanted you.' The last three words were added more softly, consideringly, and she felt a delightful shiver touch her spine, and smiled at what she knew to be the truth.

'You're pretty wonderful yourself,' she answered

gently, her own eyes upon his face, shining with the light of love. 'In so many ways—not least the way you can tear people's hearts with words—the words you write.'

'Perhaps—always for you,' he told her. 'There's always been a picture of you in my mind when I started to write a play. There's a part of you in every one, did you but know it.'

'When did you first start writing?' she asked.

Lachlan shrugged. 'When I was a boy. But I was careful to keep quiet about it. I must have sensed, even then, that writers were "different" people. I used to write kids' stories when I was eight or nine —and hide them at the back of an old cupboard where no one ever looked.' He laughed. 'I dare say there's still a bundle of faded paper with the childish scribble on if I look.'

'I'd like to see.'

'You will—when we return home, my love.' He rested his fingers on the pulse that beat at her throat, and stroked her neck gently. 'Mmm,' he murmured. 'So soft, so warm—so feminine.' He leaned forward and kissed her lips, and Catriona closed her eyes. It was a short, sweet-tasting kiss, and when it was done he leaned back slightly. 'I needed that,' he whispered. 'Just to kiss you, to remind myself how wonderful you are.'

Catriona stroked his cheek, then rested her hand on it, smoothing back the hair, the thick black hair she so loved to touch. 'I think I can stand that,' she agreed, as if considering it.

'You'd better,' he growled. He turned his face slightly, kissed the palm of her hand. 'Or it'll be a beating for you.'

'Promises, promises,' she giggled.

He laughed, leaned forward to hug her, and whispered in her ear: 'As if I ever could!'

'Don't spoil it,' she begged. 'I thought it might be giving you ideas for a new play. Oh, Lachlan, the one I read tonight—it's wonderful, truly. It left me absolutely shattered with the force of the emotion it roused.'

'That's the effect I want it to have.' He released her slightly, so that he could look properly at her. 'It is, in essence, a very simple love story. Yet there could be no future for them together. In a way their parting at the end is probably the most unselfish thing either of them has done.'

'That came across only too clearly,' she said. 'It made me want to weep at the sheer beauty of it.'

'They say all the greatest love stories have to have an unhappy ending,' he answered. 'Look at Abelard and Heloise—Antony and Cleopatra—tragedies, and yet—not.' He lifted her chin slightly. 'We'll be the exception, my dearest.'

'I couldn't bear it if——' Catriona stopped, shivering momentarily, and he held her closely to him.

'No, not us,' he whispered. 'Not us. Our love will go on—and on.'

'I love you so much, Lachlan.' Her voice was the faintest murmur.

'And I you. Don't you see? We were meant to come here together—as it was also meant that we should part ten years ago. Because then wasn't the time. We both had to do some growing up first. Now, now is the time for us. Now and for all the days of our lives ahead.' His voice was equally soft, and it lent potency to his words. They had a strength and force that filled her with a heady sensation, a dream-like feeling, a floating.

She could feel his heartbeats against hers. They seemed to blend into one sound. Holding each other as if they would never let go, they kissed again; this time it was more wonderful and deep than anything that had gone before, and at the end both were trembling slightly. 'Dear girl,' Lachlan said, brokenly, 'I want you so much—you must send me away now, or——' he stopped. He smiled slightly, his eyes very dark and gentle on her.

'Yes, you must go,' she whispered, but still they held each other, and both were warm with a heat that owed nothing to the fire, and both knew that the words they were saying had little meaning but had to be said. 'But not yet. Not just yet——'

'No, not yet,' he agreed, and kissed the tip of her nose, and bit it gently.

'Ouch!' she protested, and he silenced the word with his mouth, and as he did so, pushed her backwards so that she was lying down, and he with her.

Catriona eased herself slightly sideways so that he could lie comfortably beside her, and he gave a deep sigh and said: 'That's better.'

She turned her face towards him. They were in shadow now, hidden from the light, and all was quiet, save for distant thunder rumbling occasionally, not frightening, not anything save as a far away background to the rain that tapped the windows with cold fingers. 'Warm enough?' she asked.

'I could be warmer——' his voice faded away. There was a hint of laughter in it.

'Dear me, you mustn't catch cold,' she said. And he slid inside the covers, and they were together, holding each other, warm and very comfortable.

'The trouble with you,' she added, 'is that you're spoiled.'

'How true,' he murmured, and his hands left a trail of fire as he moved them around her body.

'Utterly spoiled. And what are you going to do about it?'

'I'll have to think of something,' he said, and she laughed as she buried her face in his neck.

'I'm sure you can. I'm not sure if I dare ask——' His lips came down on hers, effectively stopping what she had been about to say, then there were no more words, there was only silence, and movement, and the growing warmth that filled them both ...

They arrived back at Crannich on the afternoon of the following day, Wednesday. There was no one in to greet them. Catriona's grandfather was outside at the back, weeding, and they stood inside the comfortable dining room watching him for a few moments.

'When shall we tell them?' Catriona asked.

'Can we leave it until I get back from London?' Lachlan looked at her. 'I'll bring back some champagne and we'll celebrate properly.'

'If that's what you want,' she answered softly. She wasn't sure if she would manage, but it would be a superb surprise, and if he preferred it that way she wasn't going to argue.

'Yes, it is,' he said. 'I have a reason, and I'll tell you when I get back on Friday. Thank you.' He kissed her head.

Grandmother Forbes came in shortly afterwards, laden with shopping. Catriona and Lachlan were drinking tea in the kitchen, and both were soundly kissed.

'Did you enjoy your little visit to Farra?' she asked.

'It was lovely,' sighed Catriona.

Her grandmother looked shrewdly at her and smiled slightly. 'That's good,' she said. 'Now shoo, the both of you, and let me get dinner ready.'

'I'll go home and unpack,' said Lachlan, going to the door. 'Er—am I invited to dinner?'

Mrs Forbes snorted. 'What would you do if I said No? Of course you are. Away you go, then, Catriona can help me with the vegetables.'

When he was gone, she looked at Catriona. 'Simon phoned on Monday evening,' she told her. 'I said you'd gone away for a few days.'

'Did you say I'd gone with Lachlan?'

'Oh, I might have mentioned it.' She gave a little smile. 'He was very charming, actually. He'd rung to apologise for leaving so abruptly.'

'Had he?' Catriona felt only mild surprise. She had put him out of her mind so thoroughly that when her grandmother had just said Simon's name, she had had to think whom she meant. In a strange way, he was responsible for her present happiness, although he would never know it. Lachlan had never told her exactly why he disliked Simon so. Perhaps it was jealousy, pure and simple.

'Lachlan has to go to London for a couple of days,' said Catriona, starting to peel the carrots and potatoes that her grandmother had put in the bowl. 'But he'll be back on the weekend.'

'Aye, that's nice. We'll have a party then.'

Catriona hid a smile. So they would. It would be more than a simple party as well, but she would say nothing yet.

Dinner was a very pleasant affair. Farra had been totally different from anything she had experienced in her life, rough, bleak and rugged. She wouldn't have missed it for the world, but it was pleasant to be in her old home again—and with Lachlan sitting opposite at the table. He was amusing, a good conversationalist as well as being a good listener. It gradually became very clear to Catriona that there existed between him and the two old people a very comfortable, easy relationship. There would never in a million years have been that rapport with Simon and them. She was content just to sit there, not joining in, except when drawn in, just watching the man she loved above all. How different now from the brittle antagonism, the smouldering battle between them from that first moment, with Simon in the wood. That had been a different Lachlan, a hard forceful character, who rode roughshod over any opposition. This Lachlan was a man of great charm and personality. Simon had never seen him like this; he would not believe it possible. She didn't care what Simon thought.

They walked round the island that evening, and the weather was in strong contrast to that on Farra, cold but crystal clear, with the stars brightly scattered in the black sky. Lachlan had his arm round Catriona's waist. She had never known such contentment in her life, and told him so. 'The battles are over,' he said. 'For you—for me. You'll see.'

She smiled. 'For *you*? I can't imagine you quiet and docile!'

'God forbid!' he burst into laughter. 'I don't mean those kind of battles, love. The ones to do with playwriting are different—I mean in our private life. I only hope it doesn't spoil my writing, make me complacent and bland.'

'I can arrange for us to have a screaming row once a week, if that's what you'd prefer,' she said demurely, as if discussing some minor domestic arrangement.

'That's a thought,' he said, as if surprised. He looked down at her and grinned. 'And you could, too. You *are* fiery, you always were. Don't, for God's sake, change.'

'And you. Remember that scrap you had once with Johnny Campbell?'

'That? I'd forgotten.' Lachlan rubbed his jaw reminiscently. 'There was a character. I wonder what happened to him?'

'He's a doctor in Canada, so my grandmother informed me. She keeps in touch with all the news of the village. You were only about fifteen at the time, and I must have been about eight. It was the talk of Crannich for weeks.'

'I can't even remember what it was about. I can remember how it ended. Old Mother Grant came out with a broom and cracked us both over the head.' He winced. 'Ouch—end of fight!'

Catriona giggled. 'I know. I was watching from a safe vantage point with a school chum. I think I had a secret crush on you even then. I wanted you to win. I never liked Johnny Campbell very much. I was frightened of you getting hurt. I remember——' She stopped, and gave a little snort of laughter. 'Don't laugh, but I'd got hold of a stick, and if *he'd* won I was going to come down and hit him hard.'

'You little minx!' He looked at her gravely. 'And I never knew, until——' It was his turn to pause, and to look to her. 'Oh, Catriona, all those years— and yet who knows, perhaps if we'd been together then we might have changed, grown apart? Perhaps, after all, this is the right time for us.'

'You're right. Can I ask you something, Lachlan?'

'Of course.'

'Have you ever been in love with anyone in London?'

'In love?' He laughed. 'Good grief, no! I told

you, I've been waiting for you, my sweet.'

'But you must have—well, you know——'

'Had affairs? I told you, yes—but nothing important.' It was what he had said before. He squeezed her. 'Jealous?' he murmured.

'No, of course not—oh, well, yes, of course I am.'

'There's no need. There's no one, anywhere, like you.'

Catriona wondered who the women had been, if Lachlan had ever told them that he loved them. It was an easy phrase to say. He changed the subject, and she wondered, later, much later, why. But not then.

'Let's go back,' he said. 'Let's go to my house and have a drink, then I'll take you safely home to Grandma.'

'Sounds nice.' They began to walk back through the woods, leaves crunching underfoot. Catriona thought about him, with someone else, but only briefly. The thoughts hurt too much. Soon, they wouldn't matter, but it was still too new, too fragile. She knew it was foolish. A normal man of thirty-two could hardly be expected to have remained celibate. Perhaps, she thought, I'd be more worried if he had been, and smiled to herself as they made their way back, through the dark trees. I love you, she thought, and when they reached his house, she would tell him. But not yet, it could wait. They had all the time in the world.

Lachlan had gone home and left her, after telling her he would see her in the morning at breakfast—Grandmother having invited him. He kissed her as they stood on the steps, and said, 'I love you. Sleep well.'

'I will. Goodnight, Lachlan.' She watched him go, then closed the door and leaned against it for a moment. The house was silent, the hall light had been left on for her, and her grandparents were in bed.

She had had two small whiskies at Lachlan's and was pleasantly tired. She went into the kitchen to make herself a cup of tea, and as she put the kettle on the telephone rang in the living room. She ran to answer it before it woke the elderly couple, thinking, for one absurd moment that it would be Lachlan—until she remembered that he had no phone. 'Hello?' She was breathless from the run.

'Kate?' Only Simon called her Kate. She didn't want to speak to him.

'Hello, Simon.'

'At last! I tried half an hour ago. Your grandmother said you were out with Lachlan. What gives?'

'Nothing. What do you mean?'

'I mean, my sweet, that from hearing what deadly enemies you were one moment, it's rather a surprise to find you've gone away with him for a few days—and now out for a cosy evening.' She had forgotten that Simon had rung before and spoken to her grandmother.

'It's quite simple,' she said soothingly. He wasn't going to spoil it. 'He needed help with a play, that's all.'

'Oh well, that explains it,' he answered. The vibrations of anger carried very well down the line, and the heavy sarcasm, 'You must take me for a fool. And when, pray, are you coming back?'

'I've not decided.'

'I'll bet you've not!' His voice shook.

'Look, Simon, I'm tired. If you're going to be sarcastic we might as well hang up and talk some other time.' Her own voice had sharpened. 'You don't own me, you know.'

'That's only too obvious. He must have something. What is it? More money than me?'

'Why don't you ask him?' she snapped. 'He's going to London tomorrow—I'm sure he'd be delighted to tell you,' and she slammed the receiver down. Damn Simon, she thought, and went to make her tea. The fragile mood of wellbeing had shattered. She had seen the unpleasantness in Simon, quite suddenly. Perhaps Lachlan was right about him after all. He was right about everything else. She carried her tea up to bed, and gradually the unpleasantness of Simon's call was smoothed away with other, lovelier memories . . .

The house seemed an empty place when Lachlan had departed. Catriona helped her grandmother prepare lunch, and walked down to the village in the afternoon to get the shopping. It passed an hour or so for her, stopping to chat to various villagers,

mainly elderly, that she had known from childhood.
If she accepted all the offers of cups of tea she would
have been awash. As it was, it was difficult to refuse
hospitality, especially as most of the women wanted
to tell her of the plays they had seen her in. Catriona
felt a warmth for them, a caring. Everyone had been
so kind to her when she had come to Crannich as a
child after her parents had been killed. She had had
a secure childhood, and part of it had been due to
people like Mrs Grant, Mrs MacLeod, Lizzie Fraser
—the elderly woman into whose home she had gone
after her final visit, to the post office, for stamps to
answer some fan letters. She left Lizzie's at last—no
one ever called her anything else—and made her
way back to the house. The old woman's eyes had
been bright with curiosity as she probed gently
about Catriona and Lachlan. No one could move
anywhere without Lizzie knowing. Catriona had
parried the questions skilfully. Lizzie would know
soon enough. She would enjoy the party . . .

The afternoon passed with letter writing, and at
nearly tea time, when her grandmother had gone to
visit an elderly ill friend to take some broth and
magazines, Catriona had a bath, dressing in a long
warm hostess gown in rich blue afterwards, and
wandering downstairs. She wondered when Lachlan
would telephone, and as she did it shrilled in the
living room.

She picked it up. 'I knew it was you,' she told
him. 'Do you realise I've never spoken to you before
on the phone?'

His laughter echoed down the line. 'We'll celebrate that as well when I come back,' he said. 'How's everybody?'

'Fine. I've just had a bath. I'm missing you. How's everything down in the big city?'

'Hell without you,' he answered promptly. 'But I'm trying to be very brave. With any luck I'll be back home tomorrow evening, then we'll tell everyone. How about a party, Saturday?'

'Sounds lovely. Want me to start getting food in?'

'No. I'll buy everything we need in Edinburgh before I drive up. Let it be a surprise for the old folks. Listen, love, I have to go. I've a meeting with someone in half an hour. I'll phone you later tonight. Okay?'

'Okay, Lachlan—I love you.'

'Not as much as I love you. 'Bye, darling.'

''Bye.' Catriona hung up, and gave a little sigh. She glowed with happiness. She nearly skipped out to the kitchen, and began to prepare the vegetables for dinner. All I ever do is eat, she thought, and bit into a raw carrot as if to confirm the thought. It tasted good.

After dinner they all settled down to watch a play on television, and when the doorknocker went Catriona stood up. 'I'll get it,' she said.

'Are you expecting anyone, dear?' her grandmother asked, looking puzzled, at her husband.

'No,' he answered. 'But there's only one way to find out——' Catriona, smiling, went to open the door. It was the start of a nightmare.

A woman, holding an overnight case, stood on the step. She was tall, about thirty—or younger, it was difficult to tell. She was dark, slim and very attractive, although she wore little make-up and was rather pale.

'Good evening,' she said. 'I'm looking for Lachlan Erskine. Is he here?'

Catriona hid the shock of her words. 'No, he's not,' she said. 'He's in London.'

'Oh God!' The woman's face crumpled. She seemed as if she would faint. 'Oh no——!'

'You'd better come in,' said Catriona, and opened the door wider.

'Thank you.' The woman gave her a faint smile. 'I'm sorry I reacted like that—only you see, I've travelled all the way here *from* London today by train. I—thought he was living here——'

'He is. Not here, but near.' Catriona led her into the front room and switched on the fire. 'Sit down.' She went out, looked into the room where her grandparents sat, said: 'It's someone for Lachlan. I'll see to them,' and closed the door. She felt shocked, but she also felt slightly numbed.

The woman was sitting near the fire, her hands held out to warm. She shivered as Catriona went in, and looked up at her. 'I'm sorry, I should have introduced myself. My name's Barbara Greene. How—when will Lachlan be back?'

'Tomorrow night. Are you a friend of his?'

There was a brief pause. 'Yes,' she answered quietly. She looked at Catriona, as if puzzled, then said: 'Aren't you Kate Forbes?'

'I am.'

'How wonderful! I thought I recognised you. I've seen you in so many plays. You're a superb actress.'

'Thank you.' Catriona sat down in an easy chair. 'Why have you come up here, Miss Greene?'

The woman looked down at her hands, and sighed. 'We had a quarrel,' she said. 'Just before he moved up here.' Her lip trembled. 'I couldn't bear it any longer—not seeing—he didn't answer my letters, you see—Forgive me, I shouldn't be telling you this, but I have to tell someone——' her voice broke.

Catriona felt icy cold, as if something terrible had come into the room, something which froze her very spirit. Lachlan had said that no one mattered to him, except her. Yet this woman's distress was evident. She fought against a feeling of nausea and said: 'Why have you come *now*? Why now? If you had an—affair—and it's over——'

'Because I'm having his child.' Barbara Greene stood up and unbuttoned the long camelhair coat she wore. 'I'm four months pregnant, Miss Forbes.' Her eyes glittered with tears.

Catriona held hard on to the chair arms. The shock hit her stronger than a physical blow. The slender figure wasn't quite so slender, with her coat open. The telltale bulge, though slight, was there.

'Dear God!' she whispered, white-faced. The woman sat down again.

'Does—he know?' asked Catriona through frozen lips.

'No. He wouldn't phone—how could I——' She stopped. 'I had to see him, to tell him——'

Catriona stood up and paced the floor, too upset to think straight, and the woman watched her. 'Is there a hotel I can stay at?' she said quietly.

'No.' Catriona shook her head. 'You'd better stay here—until he returns.'

'Thank you. You're very kind.' She drooped wearily in her chair. 'I'm very tired. So many hours on the train, and the doctor's told me to rest——'

'I'll show you to a room. Have you eaten?'

'Yes, on the train. If I could have a cup of tea— or a glass of milk——'

'I'll take you up, then bring you one.' Catriona went forward and picked up the overnight bag from the carpet. She was giving the best performance of her life, only no one would ever know. She was acting normally when everything cried out in her to scream and cry. She hurt. She ached, deep inside with a terrible pain. Lachlan had loved this woman, enough to give her a child—only he didn't know that yet, because he hadn't answered her letters. She hoped she would make it up the stairs without being sick.

She went up the stairs, the woman following, led her into the spare room, showed her the bathroom and found her a clean towel. 'If there's anything else you need,' she said, 'I'll be downstairs. I'll go and get you a glass of milk.'

She returned with it and handed it to Barbara Greene, who had taken her coat off and was standing by the window. Catriona didn't want to look at her, and particularly not at that telltale thickening of the waist, but she forced herself. 'I'll see you in the morning,' she said. 'Good night.'

'Good night—and thank you so much for being kind. I appreciate your putting me up here—I don't know what I'd have done——'

'It's all right.' Catriona walked to the door. She had no number to ring Lachlan, to tell him, and she wasn't going to ask. She wasn't even sure if she would be able to speak to him. She went out and closed the door behind her, then down to tell her grandparents they had a guest. How fortunate they didn't know that Lachlan and she had been intending to get married . . .

She had just finished explaining that a woman friend of Lachlan's was sleeping the night when the telephone rang. 'I'll take it on the kitchen extension,' she said, and went out.

'Kate? Don't hang up on me, please——' Catriona slumped against the kitchen cupboard, her heart beating like a sledgehammer. She had thought it would be Lachlan, and for a split second she had been relieved that it wasn't.

'Simon?' she said.

'Yes. Look, love—I was a swine last night. I've only phoned to say I'm sorry. Don't hang up.'

'I won't,' she said wearily. 'What is it?' She wanted to cry—or die.

CHAPTER EIGHT

'I'm sorry I was such a sarcastic beast,' Simon said. He was turning on the charm. It had no effect whatsoever on Catriona, who didn't want to speak to anybody. 'I was jealous, let's face it. I thought that you and Lachlan——' he paused delicately.

She gave a hollow laugh. 'Did you? Well, you're wrong. Look Simon, I can't talk—something's cropped up.'

'Everything all right?' His voice held concern.

'Fine,' she lied. 'But I'm very tired. Don't ring me again here, I'm going away for a day or two——'

'Oh God, with *him*?' he cut in.

'No, alone. I'll ring you in a day or so.' She had no intention of doing so. She didn't even know where she was going, but she was weary of him, of everyone, especially Lachlan.

'Promise? Are you sure you're all right? You sound——'

'I'm sure,' she said. 'I'll ring you. Please—leave me——' her voice broke.

'Kate, love——'

She found control. 'I'm sorry, that was silly. I just don't feel very well. I'll phone you. Goodbye, Simon.' She hung up, and paced the kitchen, hand to burning forehead. She was going away, she knew

that now, but where to? Not Farra, not there, alone.
And not London. She made a little sound of pain
deep in her throat, and when the telephone rang a
few moments later she thought it was Simon again,
only it wasn't. It was Lachlán.

'Hello, love.' His voice, warm and loving, came
clearly over the wires. For a moment the room spun
round as Catriona struggled to regain her mental
equilibrium. Oh God, it was him! She clutched the
receiver and she couldn't speak. 'Catriona?' His
voice was sharper, questioning.

'Yes, it's me,' she said, and her voice was flat and
dead.

'What is it, love?' he asked.

'Barbara's here,' she said. 'I think you'd better
come home.' Each word was an effort.

'Barbara who?' He sounded puzzled.

For one moment, just for one moment, her heart
leapt. It was all a mistake, it must be. 'Barbara
Greene.'

There was a dreadful, heart-shattering silence.
Then: 'Oh God,' he muttered, and she knew. Her
mouth went so dry that she could scarcely speak.
'She's *there*?'

'She's sleeping here,' she managed to say. 'I
couldn't turn her out. You see, she's about to have
your child——' her mouth trembled. 'She wrote,
but you never answered her letters——'

'Catriona?' His voice cut in sharply. 'Listen to
me—get her to the phone——'

'Is it true, then? Have you had an affair with
her?'

'Yes—but listen——'

'No, you listen to me,' she said, very steadily, one part of her proud of her self-control. 'She loves you —and she's having your child——'

'I'm coming up,' he cut in. 'I'm coming up to-night.'

'Do that. She wants to see you, I don't. I won't be here when you come. Goodbye.' She replaced the receiver quietly, waited for a few moments, then took it off again. The burr of the dialling tone came loudly.

It was nine o'clock. If Finlay could be dragged away from his television to take her on the ferry, she could catch the ten o'clock train to Edinburgh. Her grandparents had two friends living there, of whom Catriona was very fond, and who would be delighted to see her. Lachlan wouldn't find her there. She would stay there until she got herself sorted out. She felt so confused and unhappy. She wanted to sleep, but she knew she couldn't remain any longer under the same roof as Lachlan's mistress. She didn't want to hurt her grandparents, but she would have to tell them the truth. They had a right to know, and when they knew, they would understand.

Taking a deep breath, she went in to tell them.

She sat on the train taking her away from Crannich, trying to read a magazine. The train was nearly empty, and the darkened countryside sped past in a blur, and Catriona sat there numbed and unfeeling. She couldn't take any more. She would never love another man, or trust one, as long as she lived. The soft clickety-clack, clickety-clack of wheels on track should have been soothing, but it wasn't. She looked out of the window, dry-eyed, unseeing. Aunty Janet and Uncle Bob Maclaren were expecting her. They would meet the train, they had told her when she had telephoned, and they had only been vaguely surprised at the lateness of the hour. Not related to her, yet she had always known them as Aunt and Uncle, they were a middle-aged childless couple who visited her grandparents often. They would be curious, but they were also tactful and kind. She wouldn't have to explain everything, only the merest details.

Her grandparents had been upset, naturally, but Catriona had sworn them to secrecy about where she was going and promised to return—as soon as Lachlan went back to London with Barbara. Then, and this had been the most difficult thing of all, Catriona had gone up to tell Barbara that Lachlan would be here the following morning.

Barbara had been reading a book in bed, the empty glass of milk on the bedside table. Catriona had told her that Lachlan was travelling overnight, and would be there after breakfast. Then she had packed a suitcase and left.

The train was due in Edinburgh at just gone one. Catriona hoped her Aunt Janet would have a sleeping pill. She was going to need one. If not, a stiff whisky, or even two.

She looked at her watch. Midnight. Another hour,

then bed, and, she hoped, oblivion for a time. She pictured Lachlan, perhaps on a sleeper, or catching a plane, travelling back to Crannich and the mother of his child. He had said he wanted children; that wish was going to come true sooner than he had expected. Catriona closed her eyes and tried to doze, but in vain.

Aunt Janet was waiting by the barrier. She kissed Catriona warmly. 'Bob's in the car,' she said. 'We'll have you home in no time. We put the electric blanket on the spare bed the minute you phoned. Come on, dear.'

'Aunt Janet,' said Catriona, as they hurried out of the station, 'I'm sorry to have sprung this on you at such short notice, but I had— problems—I had to get away——'

'Look, love, you don't have to tell us. I'm sorry you couldn't have come under pleasanter circumstances, but you know there'll always be a bed for you whenever you want it.' They reached the fawn-colored car, and Bob leaned over to open the doors.

'In you get,' he said cheerfully.

'Hello, Uncle Bob—I feel awful keeping you up like this——'

'Nonsense,' he boomed. 'You're family, aren't you? What are families for, hey?' Catriona put her head on Aunt Janet's shoulder, and sobbed helplessly. She didn't see the concerned glance that they exchanged. She didn't see anything. She had never been so unhappy in her life.

They drove her to their comfortable house on the

outskirts of Edinburgh, where a bedroom was prepared, warm and elegant, and softly lit, and Janet
took Catriona's coat from her, and as she did so
something fell from the pocket and rolled along the
carpet. Catriona bent to pick it up, and all the
memories of Farra rushed back. It was the small red
button that Lachlan had picked up from behind
the counter of the store on their first morning there.
She placed it in the ashtray on the mantelpiece. It
could be thrown away now. She wanted no souvenirs
of him or of Farra.

'Do you happen to have any sleeping pills, Aunt
Janet?' she asked.

Janet smiled. 'I'll find you something,' she said.
'And how about a hot milky drink to go with it?'

Catriona smiled. 'Yes, please,' she said. 'I can't
thank you enough——'

'Oh, tush! You heard what Bob said. He's gone
to bed already, and I don't have to be up at any
particular time in the morning, so there's no prob-
lem at all. And you will stay in bed as late as you
like, you hear me?' Catriona nodded. Their concern covered her like a warm, comforting blanket.
Aunt Janet was in her fifties, plump and reassuring,
like her husband. They had visited Catriona occasionally on their rare visits to London, and always
enjoyed meeting her show business friends. They
watched her plays, whenever she was on television,
and showed her photograph to their friends as
proudly as though she were their own daughter. She
had not visited them so often as she should have,

recently. Since she had met Simon, her life had become so much more hectic. There never seemed to have been time.

She sat on the bed and eased off her shoes. That would all change in the future. She had been selfish, she could see that clearly now, dazzled by fame, neglecting the older, truer friends, those who asked nothing yet gave of their time and affection freely. There would be no more Simon, no more Lachlan—— Life would change, but it would be one for the better, because Catriona knew that in the other way lay despair. She smiled at Janet. 'Next time you're in London,' she said, 'let me know, and I'll take you out on the town.'

'We will. Bob has to go down on business in a few weeks. We'll keep you to that.' She hung up Catriona's jacket. 'I'll go and find that pill for you. You know where the bathroom is. The pink towel's yours.' She gave Catriona a reassuring smile and vanished.

Catriona was sitting in bed when she returned. 'There you are. Swallow that with your Horlicks and you'll sleep like a top.' She sat down. 'You'll see, things will be better in the morning. They always are.'

Catriona took the pill. It seemed a sign of weakness to take one, and she never had before, but she didn't want to be awake, to think. She sipped the hot smooth drink and swallowed the pill. 'Done,' she said

Janet chuckled. 'There. Finish your drink, then

lie down. Breakfast will be whenever you wake, and want it. It's lovely having you, and we'll look after you for as long as you want to stay, Catriona, you know that.'

'I do, Aunt Janet—I'm glad I came.' She had finished the hot creamy Horlicks and snuggled down under the covers. Janet bent over to tuck her in, with a motherly gesture.

'Goodnight, dear,' she said. 'Sleep tight.'

'And you. Goodnight.' It was like being a child again, safe, warm, looked after. Catriona closed her eyes as the door was softly shut, and the room was in darkness. The pill seemed to be having its effect already, although that could have been her imagination. Whatever it was, she was feeling drowsy and extremely comfortable, and the pain was gradually easing away, away ...

She dreamt wild dreams, of running away in a mist-shrouded land, where the ground was soft and clinging, and she could scarcely move. Some nameless terror pursued her, distantly but coming nearer, ever nearer—and when she woke from that, drenched in sweat, and relieved that it had been only a dream, she fell asleep again to hear mocking laughter, and to see Lachlan and Barbara, strangely distorted, larger than in life and with faces that taunted her as they stood side by side, staring at her, laughing, enjoying a joke in which she couldn't share, until she couldn't bear it. Then the dreams changed, and became those of childhood, and she saw again the fight with Lachlan and Johnny Campbell, who changed into the young student in mid-struggle, and the dream grew distorted and painful, and she wanted to escape, but couldn't.

She woke about six, and the dreams disappeared, and for a long time she lay there afraid to sleep again, going over in her mind everything that had happened, until she was so exhausted that she could think no longer, and everything was blotted out at last in a merciful oblivion.

Then at last Catriona awoke from a deep dreamless sleep, and it was daylight. As she surfaced from slumber she thought of Lachlan, and she opened her eyes, blinking away tears that must have come during sleep. The sun streamed in through the window on to the bed.

Sitting in a chair by the window, watching her, was Lachlan. She closed her eyes again to banish the hallucination, then opened them again.

'Hello, Catriona,' he said. 'I've been waiting for you to wake up.'

She didn't know how he had got there. He didn't know, he couldn't, because both her grandparents had promised—although reluctantly—not to tell him. And even so, it was impossible for him to have travelled to Crannich and left again, because that was where he had been going—to see Barbara. It was only morning now—and he couldn't *really* be there. It was physically impossible for him to have done it. The only thing wrong with her thinking was that he *was* there. He was certainly no figment of her imagination. He was solid and real, and wore a dark suit, white shirt and grey tie—he looked completely different from how she had ever seen him before. He stood up now, and approached the bed, looking down at her. 'Nothing to say?' he enquired.

Catriona stared back at him. 'How did you get here?' she whispered.

He sat down on the bed. 'I thought you'd never ask.' His face was grim, hard, serious. 'I drove here after retrieving my car from the airport. And if you want to know *why*, it's because, after I'd taken a taxi to the airport from the train on which I'd travelled overnight from London, I telephoned Crannich.'

'They weren't supposed to tell you,' she said. 'I told them—they promised——'

'I persuaded them,' he cut in. 'I'm good at that, remember?'

'You're good at getting anything you want, I remember *that*!' she said bitterly.

'Indeed I am. Sit up, Catriona.'

'No!'

Lachlan pulled her roughly, and grabbed the pillows behind her so that she was forced to sit up. His hands weren't gentle, and she saw the deep anger in him and felt fear. It was she who should be angry, except she hurt too much to be so.

'You'll sit,' he gritted, 'because so help me, if I'm tempted to hit you—and I am—I'm not going to do it while you're lying down——'

'You wouldn't dare!' she spat, the despair changing rapidly to temper. 'If you do——'

'Yes? What will you do?' He looked at her.

'You'll regret it,' she said, voice quivering. 'You —you should be with *her*, the woman you got pregnant and conveniently forgot—is that what you do? Love 'em and leave 'em——'

She got no further. She saw his hand move, but it was too swift for her to avoid. The next second he had slapped her cheek. It stung. It hadn't been a blow, more a contemptuous tap, but it stung not only her face but her pride. Without thinking, she lashed back and landed him a hard whack on his face—and before she could even think he grabbed her and pulled her from the bed to stand upright. He shook her, his face white with temper. 'Now we're quits,' he grated. 'As yet—but by God, I'm tempted to beat hell out of you just to make you see some sense! I hope I retain enough control not to do it—but you'd better listen to me—and you'd better not fight me any more, because my patience is at an end.'

'What about *her*?' she demanded, trembling. 'Doesn't *she* count any more?'

'I said—shut up!' he pushed her on to the bed and made her sit down, 'and listen.' He pulled up a chair and sat on it. 'When *I've* finished, if you have anything to say *then*, I'd be pleased to hear it.'

'I'm not going to listen to you. Where's my aunt?' She made as if to stand up, and Lachlan pushed her down again.

'You are, you know,' he said. 'She's gone out shopping, so it's absolutely no use appealing to *her* for help.'

'She—left you here?' she gasped.

'When I told her who I was, and why I'd come, yes,' he answered. 'Are you ready to listen to me?'

Catriona put her hands to her ears. He reached out and pulled them away, then began to speak. Quietly and slowly he began to tell her, and his hands were on her wrists, so that she was held help- lessly. 'I telephoned Crannich and your grand- mother answered,' he said. 'It was breakfast time. I asked for you and she told me you'd gone away for a few days and had made her promise not to tell me where you were. All right, I said, I accept that, but will you let me speak to Barbara?' He paused. 'She went to get Barbara—incidentally, it had taken me fifteen minutes to get all the ten-pence pieces I knew I would need for the call—and I sure needed them all, all twenty of them—and after a few minutes she came back to the telephone and told me—very be- wildered she was too—that Barbara had left. It surprised *her*. It didn't surprise me. Did you tell Barbara last night that I was returning immedi- ately?'

Catriona looked at him, too dazed to answer for a moment. How could Barbara have gone? Gone where? 'Answer me,' he said.

'I don't understand,' she whispered.

'Oh, but you will, you will. *Did you tell her?*'

She nodded. 'I went up to tell her that you were coming up from London overnight, after I'd told my grandmother I was leaving,' she answered quietly, still in a whirl of confusion. It was all awry, all—wrong somehow.

'And how did she react to your bit of news? Delighted? Pleased?' he asked, his voice dry.

She had to remember. For some reason it seemed important to him. She had gone in, and Barbara had been reading a book in bed, and Catriona had said: 'Lachlan's just been on the phone. I've told him you're here and he's travelling up overnight. He'll be here about eleven——' There had been a sudden look on Barbara's face as she said the words that, then, had seemed to Catriona, in the midst of her numb despair, to be surprise. Now, after the harshness of his words, and with the rapidity of events, she could interpret that look differently. It had been—shock, more than surprise. She had made some reply, Catriona couldn't remember precisely what, but asking the time he would arrive, as if to check, as if she hadn't heard—and Catriona had answered and left her. She looked up at Lachlan now; he had sat silently watching her as she fought to remember.

'She seemed—startled,' she said.

'Startled? Wouldn't you have expected her to look relieved at seeing her "lover"—the father of her child?' he asked grimly.

'I was past thinking clearly,' she told him, her voice bitter. 'I'd had more than a few shocks myself.'

'So you had.' He nodded. 'And there's a few more

coming up. Why, tell me, should she leave this morning so suddenly?'

'I don't know,' she said dejectedly. 'I don't know anything any more.'

'Then I'll tell you,' he said. 'It's because she didn't *want* to see me. The last person she expected to see was me.'

'You're not making sense!' she burst out.

'I will do in a minute. She succeeded in what she'd set out to do—namely, get at you. She succeeded very well, didn't she? She's no more pregnant than I am.'

'I *saw* her!' Catriona snapped. 'Don't try and——'

'You saw a woman carefully padded to look pregnant, you little fool. Good God, you've been in enough plays, haven't you?'

'She was your mistress——' she cut in.

'We had a brief affair, I regret that—but I'm not trying to pretend it never happened. God, I told you I'd not been a monk.'

'She loves you.' Tears welled in her eyes. 'She—told me—you'd quarrelled.'

'She's a better bloody actress than I thought. She should be on the stage instead of designing sets if that's how well she did it. To fool *you*, and you're in the business—My God, she must have been good! I'm sorry I wasn't there to see it—only of course, if I had been it wouldn't have happened, would it?'

'She'd travelled all the way up from London *ex-*

pecting to see you!' Catriona cut in. 'She—nearly cried when I told her you'd gone to London——' She faltered. What was he saying? She couldn't take all this information in. Nothing made sense any more.

'I'll bet she nearly cried when you told her I was coming back,' Lachlan said grimly. 'Good grief, how stupid are you? Don't you realise what's been happening? It was all a set-up, and you fell for it, hook, line, and sinker. She'll be on her way back to London now to tell the man who put her up to it, to tell him it worked.'

Catriona went very cold, icily cold. He had been leading up to this, she knew that now. Everything had been leading up to this one point. White-faced, she looked at him, and he grew blurred as she fought to stop herself from fainting. 'The—man?' she queried, very quietly, her heart beating rapidly.

'Oh yes,' he nodded. 'I see that light is dawning at last. The man whom—and I'll bet a thousand pounds on this, because it's a bloody certainty—the man whom *you* told, over the phone, that I'd gone to London.'

'Simon?' she whispered.

'Yes, dear Simon. You did tell him, didn't you?' She nodded. 'And I'll also bet he phoned you again last night, to establish that she was there. Only he wouldn't ask, of course. That would be giving his pretty little game away—but he'd know by your reaction whether she was or not. Right?'

Again she nodded. He went on: 'I knew he'd be

up to something the minute he left. I knew that, because he hates my guts, and no one does what I did to Simon—or says what I said—and gets away with it.' He stood up. 'The only snag there is the fact that I don't get beaten by anyone so easily. And by him, I don't get beaten at all.' He smiled; it wasn't a pleasant smile. 'He was one of the reasons I went to London. I've set enquiries in motion— he'll regret he ever met me. And now, knowing this, he's going to regret it a damned sight more.' He tilted her chin. 'I underestimated him in one thing. I didn't think he was such a fast worker. He must have been very busy from Saturday onwards to get to Barbara so quickly.' He let go of her and moved away towards the window. 'You'd better get dressed. When you've eaten we're driving down to London.'

Catriona remained where she was, too stunned to move. Lachlan turned. 'Did you hear me?'

'Yes.'

'Then get yourself ready. It's nearly three o'clock——' She looked at her watch. Surely it was only morning? It wasn't. She must have slept on for hours after waking early. 'We're setting off soon— and you are not going to be let out of my sight for a single moment. I hope that's clear enough, Catriona.'

'We're going to see—him?' she whispered.

'Indeed we are.' Lachlan smiled thinly, and she shivered. He was implacable. He was—deadly.

'Then let me get dressed,' she said.

'I told you, I'm not leaving you for an instant. No

more running away—you can dress with me here.'

'Damn you, no, I won't!' she retorted, a spark of life returning.

'Do you want me to dress you?' he asked quietly.

She didn't answer. She stood up. 'Turn your back,' she said.

He turned away and she opened her case and found her clean underwear, and began to dress quickly, as if he might turn at any moment. But he didn't. He remained with his back to her, looking out of the window.

'I trust I can go to the bathroom alone,' she said icily.

'Indeed you can. But I'll be near.'

Catriona slammed out of the room. Dear God, why did she love him? He was a man of steel, ruthless and devastating. He must hate her now, his only desire for revenge. She felt sick at that thought.

When she had washed, and returned to the bedroom, he was there, still waiting. He held the red button in his hand and looked at her. 'Throwing away your souvenir of Farra?' he enquired.

'There's no reason to keep it,' she answered. Lachlan replaced it in the ash tray.

'Of course not.'

She closed her case and locked it, and stripped the sheets off the bed. He made no attempt to help her, simply watched her. When she had finished, and the sheets were folded neatly, he said: 'Your aunt has just returned. We'll go down.'

He picked up her case, and Catriona took her

jacket from the door and went out, followed by the dark silent stranger whom she didn't know at all.

'You will phone your grandparents before we leave,' he said, as they went down the stairs, 'and tell them that you're all right, and going down to London for a day or so.'

Aunt Janet was in the kitchen, and making tea. She greeted Catriona with a beaming smile, then, seeing Lachlan with her case, said: 'Oh! Not leaving already?'

'Mrs Maclaren,' said Lachlan, with a warm friendly smile, 'we have to go down to London for a short time, to sort out a few—things. I hope you don't mind?'

She blushed slightly, reeling under the impact of his charm. 'Of course not,' she said girlishly. 'Dear me, of course not. Now, Catriona, you must be hungry, dear, what would you like?'

'Just a piece of toast, Aunty,' said Catriona.

'Are you sure?'

'We'll be eating on the way down,' Lachlan explained. 'We're driving there.'

'Oh, well, in that case——' Aunt Janet put a slice of bread in the toaster. 'Do sit down, Mr Erskine——'

'Lachlan, please,' he cut in, smooth as butter.

'Lachlan, then. Will you have a cup of tea?'

'I'd love one.' He sat opposite Catriona. And Janet had her back to them, pouring boiling water into the teapot. He looked at her and there was no love in his eyes now. Nothing. He had replaced the

little button in the tray when she had said that
there was no reason to keep it. 'Of course not,' he
had said. Catriona's mouth was dry. That was what
he meant. It was all over. She didn't want to go to
London with him. She didn't want to go anywhere.
But she knew, beyond any doubt, that he would
take her by force if necessary, and there was simply
no point in resisting. She had no weapons to fight
him, none at all. He was a man without mercy.

CHAPTER NINE

HE drove away from the house, switching on the radio as they reached the end of the road. Catriona's case was in the trunk and her jacket was on the back seat. They had said their goodbyes to Aunt Janet, who had managed to hide well any confusion she felt, and kissed them both warmly and told them to go and see her again soon. 'We will,' Lachlan had assured her, and Catriona had watched him, knowing the truth. She would be alone when next she visited them.

He didn't speak at all until they were on the M6 motorway. The music effectively dispersed the brittle silence in the car, and he turned it down as he said:

'Do you want to eat yet?'

'No, thank you.'

'Then we'll stop for dinner about eight. I want to get as far as possible on our way before we halt.' He spared her a brief glance. 'We'll be in London before midnight.'

'Will we?' she asked listlessly. 'You don't know where I live, do you?'

'No. And I don't need to. We'll stay at my apartment.'

Catriona caught her breath. 'Why?'

'I told you, I'm not letting you out of my sight.'

She didn't say any more. There was no point in arguing with him, none at all. The barrier that was between them seemed to grow with every mile that passed. Only a day or so ago it would have been the most wonderful thing in the world to be going down with him to his apartment. She smiled to herself, a wry little smile. Now, nothing. She had no more tears to shed, no more emotions within her, only a dull grey sense of desolation. She knew she would, and had to, fight back. But not yet. Not just yet. Soon, when it was all finally over. She took a deep breath, seeing the traffic that they passed being left behind as if at a standstill. They were in the fast lane, and Lachlan drove at over eighty miles an hour, steadily eating up the miles in the powerful car, his hands firm on the wheel, his face hard. There was a police car in the distance ahead, and he eased off the accelerator until they were doing a sedate and steady seventy. When it was safely passed, the speedometer needle crept up again.

It grew dark, and now the lights of cars shone out, beaming a path, and the oncoming traffic the other side of the central barrier was a Morse code of glittering lights. It had begun to rain, and he switched on the windscreen wipers and they made a soft whirring sound, almost soothing, almost hypnotic.

Catriona closed her eyes, lulled by the rhythm, and must have dozed off, for the next thing she knew, they were slowing down and Lachlan was saying: 'Wake up. We're here.'

They were in the car park of a hotel, not a motorway service station. 'Where are we?' she asked.

'Somewhere in Staffordshire, about a mile from the motorway. Get out.'

She opened the door, and he locked it after her, then got out himself. The hotel was a long, rambling building: 'The Peacock Hotel', the sign proclaimed. It was fairly full, and everyone stared when they went in, and Catriona experienced the usual reaction she had nearly everywhere, faint recognition, the 'haven't—I—seen—her—somewhere—before?' look she knew so well.

'I want to go to the Ladies',' she said.

'Certainly. Down that corridor.' Lachlan pointed. He had been here before, obviously, for a man came up as he was pointing.

'Good evening, sir. Dinner for two?'

'Please.'

'If you'll sit in the lounge, I'll bring you a menu. Drinks?'

'Yes, please. Whisky and water for me. Catriona, what would you like to drink?'

'Vodka and orange, please.' She walked away.

He was sitting at a table studying a menu when she returned. Two glasses were on the table. She sat down, picked up hers, and drank it.

'Can I have another one?' she said.

Lachlan raised an eyebrow. His glass was still untouched. 'That was a double,' he remarked.

'Was it? Can I have another one, or are they rationed?'

He raised his hand, beckoned a waiter and pointed to her glass. The waiter nodded and went away. 'Going to get drunk?' he asked.

'If I possibly can.' She looked at him and smiled pleasantly. 'It seems a good idea at this moment.' She paused. 'You don't need to worry. I won't stand up on the table and start doing a strip-tease—though I'm sure it wouldn't bother you if I did.'

'You'd find out if you tried it,' he said, and handed her the menu. 'Why don't you decide what you'd like to eat?'

'I don't want anything to eat. I'm not hungry.' She glanced down the lists of courses, completely uninterested, and shrugged. 'I'll have an omelette.'

'Very well.' The waiter returned with her drink, and Lachlan ordered an omelette for Catriona and steak and salad for himself.

She wanted to hurt him—she wanted to tell him she loved him—she didn't know which she wanted most. The drink was helping, blurring the pain somewhat, and warming her. With her empty stomach, it was also having a more rapid effect. Her face felt as if it were glowing, and her head was beginning to feel muzzy. She drank her second vodka more slowly, and when they went into the dining room, had another one with her omelette. She merely toyed with that, leaving half, and she didn't know or care whether it was delicious or not.

Lachlan had only the one whisky, and after his steak he had cheese and biscuits; Catriona wanted nothing.

She stumbled as they went outside into the cold rain, and he put his hand under her arm. 'You'd better sit in the back,' he said. 'Lie down and try to sleep.'

It seemed an admirable idea, and she crawled in, put the coat beneath her head as a pillow, and closed her eyes. She was hazily aware of a door slamming, the throb of the engine, but it was all quite distant and far away. It didn't seem to concern her at all. The heater was on, and the car became warm very quickly, and the sound of the wipers, and of the engine, became a soothing lullaby. She fell asleep within minutes of them seting off.

When she woke up it was pitch black, the car was still and silent, and Lachlan was shaking her arm. Her head ached, and she felt stiff all over; she looked up at the shadowy blur of him as he leaned in the car, and uttered the immortal words: 'Where am I?'

'In my garage. Come on, out you get. You've slept all the way.' Catriona struggled to ease herself out, and looked outside to see a quiet street, shadowed, empty, a block of flats to the left with one lamp burning outside, showing the sign: 'Langdale Court'.

She knew where she was. She was about a mile from where she herself lived. Lachlan had her case, and he took her arm to guide her out, then locked the garage door. Their footsteps echoed across the

empty pavements and the air was very cold so that
her breath became steam. There was a distant hum
of traffic, but here all was quiet.

They went up in an elevator, and out along a thick
carpeted corridor until he reached a door, which he
opened, pushed her gently in, and then locked. She
heard the double 'click' and knew what kind of lock
it was. It could only be opened with a key. They were
in a hallway leading into a room.

The lights came on, and she looked round the
room in which they stood. No doubt about it, it was
a man's room, elegant but austere, a desk and typewriter by the window, a bookcase near it, a three-
piece suite and thick carpet. The furniture was old
and beautiful, the carpet a deep maroon with gold
pattern on it. The undrawn curtains were floor-
length brown velvet. 'Sit down,' said Lachlan. 'I'll
get us a drink. More vodka?' He went over to draw
the curtains as he spoke, and Catriona took off her
shoes and sat down on the brown leather settee. It
smelt of polish, and the faintest aroma of good
cigars.

'Yes, please,' she answered. 'You have a lovely
place. How big is it?'

'This room—kitchen—bathroom—two bed-
rooms. Were you worried there might be only one?'

The thought had crossed her mind. 'Not at all,'
she said coolly. The sleep had done her good. She
felt wide awake and comparatively sober. 'I was
merely making conversation.'

He took off his jacket and flung it over a chair,

then went and took out a bottle and two glasses from a sideboard. This would probably have been where they would have lived, if ...

'Thank you.' She took the glass from him and drank the contents in one swallow, and nearly choked. It was neat vodka.

'I was about to ask you if you wanted tonic or anything with it,' he said drily. Catriona took a deep breath. Her eyes were watering with the shock. She handed him the glass.

'Tonic, please.'

'On its own?'

'No, with more vodka.'

'Are you sure you can take it?'

'Try me,' she shrugged.

'I don't know what you're trying to prove,' he commented.

'I'm not trying to prove anything,' she answered, careful to enunciate her words clearly. 'Except that perhaps it makes it easier to bear your company when my mind is deadened by alcohol.'

Lachlan poured out a very small measure, added a liberal amount of tonic, and handed it to her. As he did so the telephone rang. He looked at it for a moment, then at her, but made no move to answer it.

Catriona sipped her drink. 'The phone's ringing,' she said brightly, and started to laugh, amused at her own wit.

'I can hear it.'

'Aren't you going to see who's calling? It might

be one of your mistresses,' she said, her mouth moving in contempt.

'And it might be someone who wants to know where I am.' He sipped his drink slowly, apparently enjoying it.

The telephone stopped as abruptly as it had begun, and the silence washed back. It was almost midnight.

'I want to be up early in the morning,' Lachlan said. 'So the sooner we get to bed, the better.'

'Why?'

'You'll see. I'll show you the bathroom and your bedroom when you've drunk that.' He raised his glass and looked at the light through it, as if admiring the heavy crystal. Catriona stroked her glass with a delicate finger.

'We're going somewhere?'

'Yes.'

'I won't ask where.'

'No, don't bother, because I wouldn't tell you anyway.'

She put her glass down on a table and stood up. 'I'm ready. I don't want any more.'

'This way.' He indicated the door to the hallway, and she followed him out. There were four doors leading off, two either side. He opened the second, and it was a small bedroom with a double bed. 'The bathroom is the one opposite,' he said. 'Is there anything else you need?'

'No.' He lifted her case in from the hallway and put it by the bed, then went out. Catriona was alone, and she looked around her.

The furnishings were plain but elegant, of blonde wood, with a matching cream carpet. The bedspread was the one bright splash of colour in the room, being of bright rose pink. She turned it down and pressed the bed, not because she cared whether it was soft or hard, but more as a reflex action. She undressed and laid her clothes neatly over a chair, put on nightie and dressing gown, found her toothbrush and went to the bathroom. The door to the living room was closed when she came out quietly some minutes later. There was a faint noise, a voice speaking very quietly. Lachlan's voice. She walked towards the closed door and stood outside it, not caring if she was eavesdropping or not. He must be on the telephone, for no one had come in.

She couldn't distinguish any words at first, so quietly was he speaking, then she heard: 'Yes, I know—it's the first chance I've had.' There was a long pause. Then: 'I see.' Another interval, then: 'That's fine. You're doing well, Simon—I'll phone you tomorrow——' Catriona heard no more. Simon? *Simon? What* was going on? She burst in, marched over to him and tried to wrest the receiver from him. Lachlan held her off easily, face showing shock for only a brief moment before turning away from her. 'I've got to go.'

'Give that to me,' she said, voice trembling, hitting him—she heard him say goodbye, and hang up, then he turned to her and grabbed both her hands. Incensed, she kicked him on the shin, and arched her body to escape, struggling violently as he sought to restrain her.

'What the *hell*——' he began.

'I heard you,' she panted, 'talking to *Simon*—What gives?'

'Hold on, you little firebrand!' he grated. 'Ouch—you little bitch!' This as she wrenched herself free and began to pummel him with all her strength, fists flailing on his chest, shoulders, arms——

He brought both his arms out and clapped them round her in a steel band that was suddenly unbreakable, and she struggled fiercely but vainly now to free herself. Exhausted, gasping for breath, her hair tumbling around her face, she went limp and still in his arms. The vodka she had drunk had taken its toll, belatedly. Heart beating as rapidly as an imprisoned bird's, she stared at him, white-faced, spent.

'There are more Simons than one in this world,' he grated, 'you violent little bitch——'

'I'm not! Don't lie to me! You were talking to Simon—Why else would you be whispering?' she hissed. She was trembling helplessly.

'I was whispering, as you call it, because my call was private, and didn't concern *you*,' he said crushingly.

'Hah!'

'God, you're an infuriating woman,' he snapped. 'You really are—Why I bother to tell you I don't know——'

'You've told me *nothing*!' she spat back. 'You drag me down here like a—like a damned parcel—and I'm supposed to behave myself. I hate you, d'you hear? You're a loathsome beast, a—a——'

'Save your language—you're going to bed right now. I've had enough—more than enough. I've tried. Thanks to you I had about two hours' sleep last night, and I don't intend that to happen again. And it's no use you trying to get out of this flat, the door's got a deadlock on it——'

Catriona stopped wriggling. He had put the keys in his pocket when he had opened the door. She had been barely aware of it at the time, but now it came back to her with some clarity. She was not going to sleep there, that was definite. There would be a time when he went to the bathroom—she had only to lift the keys, wait until he slept, and go. She had her own apartment keys with her, in her bag. 'Let me go,' she said wearily. 'I know when I'm beaten.'

'You could have fooled me,' Lachlan released her, and she walked out, the picture of a defeated woman. She wasn't aware that he watched her go, couldn't see the expression on his face.

She went into the bedroom, closed the door, and stood behind it, listening. Her ears were acutely tuned to pick up his every movement. She heard the lights click in the living room, a door close, then another open. She waited, counting slowly. She had reached twenty when she heard his quiet steps in the hall, the bathroom door opening, then closing, and the tiny click as the bolt locked. She opened her door with infinite slowness, and heard the taps running in the bathroom.

This now was her chance. Moving like a wraith, she glided across the hall and into the bedroom. His suit was on a chair, trousers under jacket, shirt and tie folded on the seat. She felt in the first pocket, and there were only a handkerchief and some coins. Then the second, and all the while her heart hammered erratically. Her fingers closed over the keys and she took them out, smoothed down the pocket, folded the jacket back exactly as it had been, and fled.

She looked at the keys in her room, and smiled. Wait until he was asleep, and leave. She could wait, now. There was all the time in the world.

Minutes passed. Lachlan left the bathroom and went into his bedroom. This was the danger moment. If he looked now, if he discovered his keys gone, he would be in straight away. Mouth dry, she waited, tense and nervous, her hands clasped, damp with perspiration. Minutes went slowly by and she counted the seconds, and each one that passed was taking her further from discovery and nearer to escape. She had left her door slightly ajar, as had he. She heard the soft swish as bedcovers were pulled back, then the faint creak of the mattress. And still she waited, breathing as quickly as she could, willing him to fall asleep quickly.

She had counted to a thousand now, and all was silent in the flat. Now—now was the time to move. She had switched her light off, and the undrawn curtains let in enough light from a distant street lamp for her to see to dress by. She stood up and eased off her dressing gown and laid it on the bed. Each movement was a step towards escape. Her nightgown was silky, and rustled when she lifted it, and she eased that off too, with infinite slowness. Arms, neck, head, over, put on bed.

She tiptoed across to her clothes, found her bra and picked it up, each movement slow and considered and——

Crash! The door was flung open. Lachlan stood there and Catriona instinctively covered herself with her hands, shocked beyond words at the violence of his entry.

'Well, well,' he drawled, and he came in and closed the door behind him. 'So you did it after all. That's it. That's *it*.' He wore a dressing gown, and apparently nothing underneath. She could only see the vague blur of him as she turned, to try and snatch her own dressing gown from the bed, but he moved very swiftly and caught her. His breathing was rapid and shallow. His voice shook. 'Oh no, you don't,' he grated. 'You're not going to escape now. I'm staying with you——' She tried to push him away, but he held her. She could feel the towering rage that filled him, could sense the leashed violence as he took her in his arms and kissed her with a savagery she had never known. Her legs buckled beneath her, she was suffocated

by his nearness, by the strength of his hands on her
body as he held her bare skin as if he would crush
her. She felt the room spin round.

'Lachlan,' she gasped weakly, as his mouth released hers for a moment. 'Oh, please—no——!'

'You've driven me mad,' he muttered harshly,
and shrugged off his dressing gown, and she
struggled vainly to escape as the robe fell to the
carpet. Dear God—he wore only brief pants——
'No—please, no,' she gasped. 'I'll do anything—
you can have the k—keys——'

'It's too late. It's much too late,' he muttered,
and as their bodies touched the heat was like a
burning fire. His legs against hers, long and hard,
so hard, his body pressed against her—she was too
weak to resist, and felt herself sliding, sliding, then
he flung her on the bed and was over her, pressing
her down into the soft yielding mattress, a heavy
dark shadow that had her pinned helplessly with
his body, legs, arms.

He began to kiss her, groaning, beyond all control, beyond all stopping, and his excitement was
so intense that she found herself helplessly respond-
ing to his savage lovemaking as his hands skilfully
tormented her weak, unresisting body.

'Dear God, no,' she gasped, but it was a token
protest, no more. The fire was kindled in her, too,
now, and the intense excitement blurred her senses
to all reason; she cried out, she knew not what,
then was silenced. The flame leapt higher, to con-
sume them both, and she was lost, lost.

*

It was early when Catriona awoke, barely seven, and she was alone. She could hear water running in the bathroom, and Lachlan whistling. She lay there very still, remembering what had happened, wondering how she could ever escape from him now. She didn't want to. Whatever transpired today, it was too late for her. The love she thought had turned to hate had been transmuted into a deeper awareness of him. She had never known what love really was before now. Her whole being was tuned to his needs and desires. She knew now, belatedly, the meaning of the play that he said he had written for her, knew the feelings that had driven the actress to the island to seek the final solution for her problems.

How had Lachlan known? How could he have written and searched the very depths of a woman's soul? He, a man? She didn't know, but then there was so much she didn't know, and probably never would, about him.

She got out of bed and put her dressing gown on, belting it firmly. Then she padded out into the kitchen and began to look for coffee, and food. There was half a loaf, and some butter in a cupboard. There was a pint of milk in the refrigerator, and little else. He had presumably intended eating out on his stay in London. She switched on the kettle and the toaster, and found plates and cutlery.

Lachlan came in as she was buttering the toast. He was fully dressed, shaved, and his hair was damp, as though he had washed it and towelled it dry. For a moment he stood in the doorway.

'I'm getting breakfast,' she said. 'But I can't find any coffee.' Her voice was even and controlled. She didn't know how he was going to be. Although she trembled inwardly, she hid it well, looking at the toaster as if it were the only thing that mattered.

'In the cupboard. I'm sorry there's not much to eat.'

'It's quite all right.' They were like strangers. Lachlan's face was serious, his voice and tone polite.

Catriona buttered the toast and put two more slices in the toaster. The kettle was boiling and she took it away from the gas and switched it off. 'What time are we leaving?' she asked.

'Now. Go and get dressed. I'll butter your toast and make the coffee.'

She went out silently. The barriers were up again, only stronger than before. This—how could this be the man who had made love to her? She washed and dressed in record time and went back into the kitchen. Her toast and coffee waited on the table. Lachlan had finished his and was rinsing his plate and cup.

She didn't feel hungry, but if she didn't eat she would be ill. She sat down and swallowed some coffee before tackling the toast. Through the window she could see that it was raining, a steady downpour. She could scarcely get the toast down; it was like trying to eat ashes. She ate one slice and left the second.

'You should eat something,' he said, hardly as if he were concerned, more a polite statement. He switched the toaster off.

'I will later. I'm not very hungry,' she said.

'Are you ready to go?'

She looked up at him. He was putting on his jacket. 'Yes,' she said.

'Where are my keys?'

'In my bedroom.'

'I'll get them.' He walked out, and Catriona, after finishing the coffee, followed. She put on her jacket and waited in the hall. Where were they going? He hadn't asked her where Simon lived.

He opened the door, double locked it behind them, and they walked to the elevator. The building was silent. The elevator whirred quietly down and he opened the front door.

'Stay there,' he said. 'I'll get the car.' It was as if he knew she wouldn't run away. Catriona waited on the steps, and when she heard the engine, went down, dashed across the wet pavement as he opened her door, and slid in. He drove in silence, no radio, no conversation. She sat looking straight ahead like a robot, still, unmoving, numbed into silence.

The traffic on the main roads was building up, and he weaved swiftly into it, and along, while she looked out, seeing the early morning workers scuttling along under umbrellas or in raincoats, and it was all unreal, like a scene in a film. She didn't seem to be part of it. It was like being in a strange city in a strange land.

Then they were turning, going down a quiet road, with cars lining the sides, and the large old houses proclaiming by their rows of door bells and little white cards that they were flats. Lachlan parked half way down, behind a Volkswagen, and said: 'This is where we get out.'

She did so, looked up at the house they were outside; it was like all the others—a little grim and forbidding, paint peeling from the door.

'This way,' he said, and walked along the pavements, seemingly oblivious of the rain that was drenching him, soaking into his suit, darkening it. She followed, and he went down a passageway into the next street. The houses here were similar but better kept. Catriona no longer knew, or cared, how far they were walking. She had a headache, and her legs were like jelly, but she followed him until he went up a path, hesitated, then went after him.

He opened the front door, which wasn't locked, and went quietly up the carpeted stairs, along a passage, and knocked at a door. Catriona followed.

'Post,' he called. 'Recorded delivery.' His voice sounded slightly different. She was behind him, and heard the rattle of a bolt, and the door opened an inch. A familiar face appeared in the crack, then——

'Oh no!' The woman tried to shut it again, but Lachlan had his foot in, then his arm, and it was swung wide open as Barbara Greene went reeling back, hand at throat, eyes wide with horror.

Catriona walked in after him. Now, at last, she knew. The room was large, elegantly furnished with a studio couch upon the back of which was a huge patchwork blanket. The room was light and airy.

'What the hell are you doing here?' gasped Barbara, and Catriona looked at her, seeing her as though for the first time. Seeing her properly at last. She wore a brightly patterned kimono and slippers. Her eyes darted to Catriona, and they were filled with hate. There was another door, ajar, near the fireplace. It moved, very slightly, as if in a breeze, but there was no wind.

'Can't you guess?' said Lachlan. He looked round him contemptuously. 'I knew you'd come back here. You're not very clever, are you?'

'Get out before I call the police,' snapped Barbara. Her eyes flickered on Catriona. 'And take *her* with you!'

'We're not going until you've told us the meaning of your sick little charade on Crannich,' said Lachlan evenly. 'And if you go near the phone I'll rip it out.'

'Big talk!' Barbara sneered. 'You don't frighten me. You can go to hell, both of you!'

'I'll give you one minute,' he drawled. 'I mean it. You'll wish you'd talked then.' His face was white, his eyes like stone, and Catriona shuddered. 'How much did he pay you?'

'I don't know what you're talking about,' she said.

'Simon Meredith is what I'm talking about,' he

answered. Then he moved. He moved very quickly,
silently across the room towards the door, and
Catriona heard Barbara shout:

'*Mind!*'

The bedroom door crashed open, and Lachlan
had gone—and as Barbara ran towards the phone,
she heard his voice. 'I should have known you'd be
here,' he grated. 'It saves me another journey——'

Simon staggered out, pulling on trousers, bare-
foot, hopping, face white with shock. Catriona saw
Barbara pick up the telephone, and acting on
instinct, rushed forward and snatched it from her.
She nearly went sprawling as Barbara whirled
round and struck out, and then, totally angry,
hurting, aching, Catriona slapped the woman hard.
Barbara fell on to the settee as Simon limped forward towards Catriona, arm upraised, eyes filled
with rage.

She backed, fearful, and the next moment Simon
too went sprawling, poleaxed by a single blow from
Lachlan's fist. He hauled him up and flung him
on the settee beside Barbara, who was holding her
chin and moaning softly.

Lachlan turned to Catriona. 'Lock the door,' he
said. 'I haven't even begun with these two.' She
obeyed, fingers fumbling at the bolt, and remained
by the door. Lachlan looked down at the frightened
couple, Simon dazed, Barbara venomous, and
smiled grimly.

'Right,' he said. 'You'd better get talking—I
don't care which one starts. But I'll warn you now,

we're not leaving until we've heard the truth behind your little caper. And you, Meredith, don't give me any excuse, because I'd like to beat you to pulp, and I warn you, I will, if I don't get the answers.' He was breathing hard, and he seemed to have grown taller, bigger. He dominated the room. Catriona didn't know what effect he was having on them, but he terrified her. She ran her tongue along her lips, leaned on the door, and waited.

CHAPTER TEN

THE story came pouring out—from Barbara. She had looked up at Lachlan, seen his face, gone whiter, if that were possible, and started talking.

She made it sound so simple and straightforward, as though it were a joke, no more. Simon had telephoned her, introduced himself as a friend of a friend, invited her out, and charmed her. She didn't look at him as she spoke. He had given her two hundred pounds, and she had agreed because— and this was with a defiant, half fearful look at Lachlan—she had wanted to get back at him for finishing with her several months previously.

He had cut in then: 'I finished with you, Barbara, because I didn't like the crowd you were mixing with—any more than I like Simon's friends. You're well suited to each other.' He turned to Catriona. 'Come on, I've heard enough. I hope you have?'

She nodded. He turned back to the sullen pair. 'Don't try any more tricks. I'm giving you fair warning now. You'll regret it more than you've ever regretted anything if you do.' He unbolted the door. 'One last thing, Meredith. Be very careful from now on.' He gave a thin smile. 'You're not the only one who can go around checking up on people. I hope I make myself clear?'

Simon's mouth opened. He seemed about to say something, clearly thought better of it, and closed it again. 'I see you understand,' said Lachlan softly. 'That's good.'

He went out after Catriona and closed the door. Dazed, she walked along the passage towards the stairs. She knew so much more now than she had. She was nearly crying with exhaustion and hunger and a sense of desolation.

Lachlan looked at her as they got into the car. 'I'm going to buy some food,' he told her, 'and then we're going home.'

'Home,' he said, as if it were hers too. But it wasn't. It never would be.

'I was brutal,' he explained, 'because I had to be. Because it was the only way to make you see the kind of man Simon Meredith is.'

She didn't answer. She sat back, white-faced, and closed her eyes. The car stopped, he got out. Some minutes later he was back, with a box of groceries which he put in the back.

When they reached the apartment he left the car outside and took her in. She felt him push her on to the settee, and obeyed, without resistance. She was numbed and cold.

Then he knelt in front of her. 'Catriona,' he said. She opened her eyes.

'Yes?'

'It's going to be all right,' he said gently, and caught hold of her hand. 'You're freezing!'

'I know.' He moved away and switched on the gas fire in the hearth. Warmth filled the room instantly. 'How can you say it's going to be all right?' she whispered. 'How can you? Don't you see— You mustn't say things like that.' She looked up at him standing there, and he was big— so big, so powerful. He would let her go soon. He had proved his point, made her see why he had brought her here. That was all he had wanted to do, and soon she could be gone. She could go back to Crannich, because that was where her grandparents were, and she had promised them. She hoped he would stay in London for a while. After that it didn't matter. When she visited them in future she would be sure to keep well away from him. He might even change his mind and decide not to live there now. Even though he owned houses there, he might not live there. He had promised her grandparents they could live in their old house, even though it was now his.

'Don't sell that house, will you?' she said suddenly.

He crouched down again. 'What?' he asked.

'My grandparents' house. Don't sell it—please!'

Lachlan frowned. 'I'm not going to. I thought I'd told you that.' He looked at her as if she had gone mad. Perhaps I have, she thought. Perhaps I'm rambling, suffering from hallucinations or something. Nothing seemed real.

She shook her head. 'I was—worried,' she said.

'I think you should go and lie down for a while.'

She closed her eyes. There was no cure for what ailed her, she knew that. 'I'm all right here, thank you,' she answered formally.

'You don't look all right. You look ill to me.'

'Are you surprised?' Tears glistened on her eyelashes, and she saw him catch his breath, saw a muscle move in his cheek. 'Don't you think I've been through enough these last few days to last a lifetime? It was only a week ago—no, slightly less, that I went back to Crannich for a—a rest—and met you again.' Her voice shook. 'Dear God, I went for a *rest*!'

'Catriona, come and lie down. We'll talk when you're feeling better.' His voice was gentle. She didn't want him being gentle. She didn't want his pity. His anger, the violence that had erupted less than an hour before—she could cope with that, but not his pity.

'When I feel better, I'm leaving here,' she answered. 'I think it's best, don't you?'

'Not without me,' he said. 'Don't you understand?'

'What do you want? Blood?' Her voice shook. 'We'll destroy one another—no, that's wrong. You'll destroy me. Nothing can touch you, can it? Nothing. You said you loved me—two days ago you told me you loved me, but you don't love anyone, perhaps not even yourself. Don't you see? I'm made of flesh and blood, not steel, like you.' Her face felt as if it was drained of all colour. She didn't want ever to look in a mirror again, for she knew what she would see—an empty, haunted face.

She put her head in her hands. 'Don't you see?' she muttered. 'You wrote that play, and I could see myself in it—and it could haunt me, for the picture you paint is too painful for comfort—but it's as though you're acting it out, as if you're changing me into *her*—you're——' She stopped, and shook her head. 'Oh, I can't—I can't!'

'Is that it? The play?' he said harshly.

'Yes—but everything else as well. I—it seems as if——'

'Wait,' he said. 'Just wait. Don't speak.' He moved away and she heard a case being opened, the rustle of paper, and then his voice again. 'Catriona, look at me, please.'

She looked up. He was holding a sheaf of type-written sheets. 'It's here,' he said.

She shivered. 'I know.'

'This is the copy as I wrote it, sweated over it, typed into the night on Crannich. This is the only copy of it in existence. Do you understand?'

She nodded, dumbly. Lachlan walked away again, towards his desk, and bent down. When he straight-ened up he was holding a metal waste paper bin. He put it on the carpet near her. 'It's finished,' he said. 'No one else will ever see it.' And he put his hands on it carefully, with great precision, and tore the entire bundle in two. He didn't look at her as he did it; his entire concentration was on what he was doing. When it was ripped across he put one half under his arm and started to tear the other half into quarters.

Then belatedly, shocked beyond measure, Catriona jumped to her feet, and held his arm. 'No, Lachlan! For God's sake, no!' she cried, her voice shaking with sheer horror. He shook her hand free and the papers ripped in two.

'Stop it, you can't——' she gasped. 'Oh God, stop!'

He looked at her then, no anger on his face, no regret at the destruction he was doing. 'I can,' he said. 'It's mine—or was. It isn't any more. It's finished. Do you think I want it now, if this is what it's done to you?'

Ashen-faced, she watched the pieces fall into the waste paper basket. The vandalism of it was more than she could bear. She sank to her knees by the bin, and Lachlan flung the last pieces in and said: 'I'm going to burn it.'

'You mustn't!' Her tears fell on the torn scraps that filled the bin. She looked at him. 'Why did you do that? I didn't mean you to do that—Oh God, it's the best thing you've ever written——'

'It's distressed you.' He pulled her to her feet and held her to him. 'Don't you know yet? Is that how you see me? As some kind of monster, using everyone? You're wrong, Catriona, just how wrong you'll probably never know—but for me, now, that play no longer exists. It's forgotten. How could I see it put on, knowing what it had done to you? I couldn't.' His voice shook. The arms that held her trembled.

'You're my life, Catriona, all I've ever wanted or needed. Dear God, what do I have to do to make you understand?' He pulled back slightly and looked at her, and she saw the glint of tears in his eyes, saw the deep dark torment on his face. 'I said I loved you because I do. I've never told any woman before that I loved her. Only you. Only you for ever and ever.' His voice broke, became deeper, huskier. 'It must be for you as well. Nothing changes —it's always been you.'

She was filled with a sudden inner strength, filled with the strength of him as he held her. She knew the truth in his words; at last she knew.

'Dear Lachlan,' she whispered. 'And we were so near to parting for ever. For it seemed as if everything had suddenly changed, and become terrible——' She shuddered. The barrier had been so real. It had been there, and growing and neither able to surmount it.

It had taken the destruction of a play to make her see the truth. For him to have done that must have taken a kind of courage she could only wonder at. 'I love you so much' she whispered. 'I always have, I always will—but I thought your love had turned to hate.'

He managed to smile—a slight one but a smile nevertheless. 'It was anger—at what he'd tried to do—and, I suppose, anger at you for even believing for one minute——' he sighed. 'Yes, I was angry with you, and deeply hurt—but I never for one moment felt my love for you falter. How could it? You're part of me, more a part of me than any play I could ever write.'

She looked down at the bin containing the pathetic shreds of paper, all that were left. 'I'm not going to let you destroy it,' she said. 'If it takes me a week, I'll piece every scrap together with Sello-tape——'

Lachlan laughed softly. 'I believe you would!'

She looked up at him. 'I mean it.'

'I won't *let* you——'

'But don't you see? It's all right now. Now that we know. It was just before—that seemed to me to be the symbol of my unhappiness, as if you'd made it happen——'

'That's why I won't let you. It's gone. Let it be.'

Catriona pulled away from him. The colour had come back to her cheeks again. 'I'm telling you——' she began.

'You don't *tell* me anything,' he said. 'Just remember that.'

'Oh, don't I?' She smoothed her hair back from her eyes. 'You'll burn that play over *my dead body*!'

'You've made a remarkable recovery,' he remarked.

She laughed. 'So I have! I'm alive—I feel—I feel better than I have for years!' She hugged him, and his arms closed round her, warm, safe, comforting.

'Oh, Catriona,' he said, burying his face in her glorious tumble of hair. 'Oh, my love, hold me like you are doing. Just hold me. I need you so much, so very much.'

She could feel his heart beating, strong, steady. She sighed a sigh of pure happiness.

'All these years,' he said, 'waiting. Not wasted, just—waiting.' He continued: 'There's a poem of John Donne's that says it all for me: "If ever any beauty I did see, which I desired, and got, t'was just a dream of thee!" There was a silence after he had said the words, then he added: 'That about sums it up for me. All the time, everywhere I went—it was you in my mind, in my heart, in my dreams.'

'And for me, too,' she answered softly. 'Always.'

It was some time later, after they had eaten and were content, and the rain had stopped and the sun shone, that Catriona knelt on the carpet in front of the fire. She had a roll of Sellotape by her, with dozens of pieces cut and stuck into the lid, waiting. She gave a deep sigh, dug into the bin, and began to spread the pieces out carefully. Tongue at corner of mouth, feeling as though she was doing a giant jigsaw, and as confused as she would be at the beginning of one, she began to piece the paper together.

Lachlan came in the room as she found a whole bundle of pieces in order and cried: 'Whoopee—look at this!' and he knelt beside her.

'I must be mad,' he sighed. 'Quite mad,' and he began the long, slow task.

'If you are, so am I,' she said. 'But there's one thing. How on *earth* do you explain this to your agent when you send him the play?' He looked at her, and his mouth quivered, then he burst out laughing.

'I hadn't thought of that,' he admitted. 'We'll have to think of something good, won't we?'

'Mice?' she suggested.

'Rats?' he said menacingly. Then they were both laughing, and he put his arm round her and kissed her, and said after a few minutes: 'Damn the play——' The piece he was holding fluttered unnoticed to the carpet, and they forgot about it for quite a while.

What readers say about Harlequin romance fiction...

"I feel as if I am in a different world every time I read a Harlequin."
A.T.,* Detroit, Michigan

"Harlequins have been my passport to the world. I have been many places without ever leaving my doorstep."
P.Z. Belvedere, Illinois

"I like Harlequin books because they tell so much about other countries."
N.G., Rouyn, Quebec

"Your books offer a world of knowledge about places and people."
L.J., New Orleans, Louisiana

"Your books turn my...life into something quite exciting."
B.M., Baldwin Park, California

"Harlequins take away the world's troubles and for a while you can live in a world of your own where love reigns supreme."

L.S.,* Beltsville, Maryland

"Thank you for bringing romance back to me."

J.W. Tehachapi, California

"I find Harlequins are the only stories on the market that give me a satisfying romance with sufficient depth without being maudlin."

C.S., Bangor, Maine

"Harlequins are magic carpets...away from pain and depression...away to other people and other countries one might never know otherwise."

H.R., Akron, Ohio

*Names available on request

HARLEQUIN SUPERROMANCE

Contemporary Love Stories

Longer, exciting, sensual and dramatic!

Here is a golden opportunity to order any or all of the first four great HARLEQUIN SUPERROMANCES

HARLEQUIN SUPERROMANCE #1
END OF INNOCENCE
Abra Taylor

They called him El Sol, golden-haired star of the bullring. Liona was proud and happy to be his fiancée...until a tragic accident threw her to the mercies of El Sol's forbidding brother, a man who despised Liona almost as much as he wanted her....

HARLEQUIN SUPERROMANCE #2
LOVE'S EMERALD FLAME
Willa Lambert

The steaming jungle of Peru was the stage for their love. Diana Green, a spirited and beautiful young journalist, who became a willing pawn in a dangerous game...and Sloane Hendriks, a lonely desperate man driven by a secret he would reveal to no one.

HARLEQUIN SUPERROMANCE #3
THE MUSIC OF PASSION
Lynda Ward

The handsome Kurt von Kleist's startling physical resemblance to her late husband both attracted and repelled Megan—because her cruel and selfish husband had left in her a legacy of fear and distrust of men. How was she now to bear staying in Kurt's Austrian home? Wouldn't Kurt inflict even more damage on Megan's heart?

HARLEQUIN SUPERROMANCE #4
LOVE BEYOND DESIRE
Rachel Palmer

Robin Hamilton, a lovely New Yorker working in Mexico, suddenly found herself enmeshed in a bitter quarrel between two brothers—one a headstrong novelist and the other a brooding archaeologist. The tension reached breaking point when Robin recognized her passionate, impossible love for one of them....

COMPLETE AND MAIL THE COUPON ON THE FOLLOWING PAGE TODAY!

HARLEQUIN SUPERROMANCE

Contemporary Love Stories

Harlequin Reader Service

In U.S.A.
MPO Box 707
Niagara Falls, NY 14302

In Canada
649 Ontario St.
Stratford, Ont. N5A 6W2

Please send me the following HARLEQUIN SUPERROMANCES. I am enclosing my check or money order for $2.50 for each copy ordered, plus 59¢ to cover postage and handling.

- ☐ #1 END OF INNOCENCE
- ☐ #2 LOVE'S EMERALD FLAME
- ☐ #3 THE MUSIC OF PASSION
- ☐ #4 LOVE BEYOND DESIRE

Number of copies checked @ $2.50 each = _____

N.Y. and Ariz. residents add appropriate sales tax $_____

Postage and handling $_____ .59

TOTAL $_____

I enclose_____ .

(Please send check or money order. We cannot be responsible for cash sent through the mail.)

Prices subject to change without notice.

NAME_____
(Please Print)

ADDRESS_____

CITY_____

STATE/PROV._____

ZIP/POSTAL CODE_____